HORNBLOWER'S
TRIUMPH

CADET EDITION OF

HORNBLOWER

IN FOUR ILLUSTRATED VOLUMES

VOLUME ONE
Hornblower Goes to Sea

VOLUME TWO
Hornblower Takes Command

VOLUME THREE
Hornblower in Captivity

VOLUME FOUR
Hornblower's Triumph

CADET EDITION: VOLUME FOUR

HORNBLOWER'S

TRIUMPH

C. S. Forester

Selected by G. P. Griggs

Illustrations by Geoffrey Whittam

LITTLE, BROWN AND COMPANY
BOSTON

The stories in this book have been selected from *Commodore Hornblower* and *Lord Hornblower*, by C. S. Forester.

CONTENTS

Summoned by the Czar

*In the spring of 1812, a year after his escape from France,
Captain Sir Horatio Hornblower, K.B., Royal Navy, was
given command, with the rank of Commodore, of a British
squadron in the Baltic. The squadron consisted of the*
Nonsuch, *a 74-gun ship, the sloops* Lotus *and* Raven, *two
bomb-ketches,* Moth *and* Harvey, *and the cutter* Clam. *The
rank of Commodore entitled him to fly a broad pendant, and
the* Nonsuch, *the only ship-of-the-line and by far the largest
in size, was the obvious vessel in which to fly it; but a stronger
reason yet for the choice was that, at Hornblower's request,
Captain William Bush, his old first lieutenant, had been*

appointed to command her. Hornblower's wooden-legged friend was thus once more at his side, and so also was his coxswain, Brown. A newcomer to his staff, with a name confusingly like that of his coxswain, was his clerk, Mr Braun, an exiled Finn who spoke a dozen languages and would serve as an interpreter also.

The British squadron arrived off the Russian naval base at Kronstadt, carrying as passengers a Swedish official, Baron Basse, and an English guards officer, Colonel Lord Wychwood, both of whom were on urgent diplomatic errands to the Russian court. The Czar was in residence at Peterhof, the palace on the Baltic shores near Kronstadt, and Bernadotte, the Crown Prince of Sweden, was his guest. Baron Basse was carrying the news of Bonaparte's invasion of Swedish Pomerania to Bernadotte, and the political scene was clouded with rumours of what Bonaparte's next move would be. The Czar and Bernadotte, the heads of the only two major powers in Europe still neutral in the struggle against French domination, were ill-assorted allies, for Russia had recently seized the Swedish province of Finland; but now a common danger had brought them together and confronted them both with the awful problem of war or peace. If it were possible to influence their decisions on whether to defy Bonaparte or submit to his threat, here was the place and now was the time.

THE brisk wind was chill, even in late May, here in the North Baltic; the squadron pitched and rolled over the short steep waves, leaden-hued under the leaden sky, as it drove ever northward towards the Gulf of Finland, towards Russia, where the destiny of the world hung in the balance. The night was hardly darker than the day, up here in the sixtieth degree of north latitude, when the sky cleared, for the sun was barely hidden below the horizon and the moon shone coldly in the pale twilight as they drove past Hoghland and hove-to in sight of Lavansaari so as to approach Kronstadt after sunrise.

Braun was on deck early, leaning against the rail, craning over in fact; that faint grey smear on the horizon to the north-ward was his native land, the Finland of lake and forest which the Czar had just conquered and from which he was a hopeless exile. Hornblower noted the dejection of the poor devil's pose and was sorry for him, even in the keen excite-ment of anticipation regarding the reception they might be accorded. Bush came bustling up, in all the glory of epaulettes and sword, darting eager glances over the deck and aloft to make quite sure that everything in the ship was ready to bear the inspection of an unfriendly power.

'Captain Bush,' said Hornblower, 'I'd be obliged if you would square away for Kronstadt.'

'Aye aye, sir.'

Hornblower would have liked to have asked if the arrange-ments for saluting were properly in train, but he forbore. He could trust Bush with any routine duty, and he had to be very careful not to interfere with the working of the ship. He was glad that so far he had never forgotten to make use of the polite forms of request when giving orders to Bush, who was his equal in substantive rank. 'I'd be obliged' and 'if you please' still came strangely enough to his lips as a preface to an order.

He turned his back on the dawn and trained his glass aft on the squadron; they were squaring away and taking up their stations astern in succession, the two sloops, and then the two bomb-vessels, and the cutter last.

'General signal,' he snapped, ' "Keep better station." '

He wanted his squadron to come up the difficult channel in exact, regular order, like beads on a string. Out of the tail of his eye he saw Basse and Wychwood come on deck, and he ignored them.

'Make that signal again,' he rasped, 'with *Harvey's* number.'

Harvey was yawing slightly from her course; young Mound, the lieutenant in command, had better keep a sharp eye on his helmsman, or he would be in trouble. There were the low grey fortifications of Kronstadt on the port bow; a turn in the channel sent the *Nonsuch* heading directly for them, so that in the event of fighting the fire of the guns there would enfilade the whole line. Then the channel swung back again, and then it straightened out so that all ships would be forced to pass close under the guns of Kronstadt. Through his glass Hornblower made out the blue and white flag of Imperial Russia flying above the grey walls.

'Make the signal "anchor," ' said Hornblower to the signal midshipman, and then he darted a meaning glance at Bush, who nodded. He had everything ready. The ship crept forward, closer and closer under the guns.

'Haul down,' said Hornblower, and the signal to anchor came down in a flash, putting the order into force at that moment. Six cables roared through six hawseholes. In the six ships a thousand men poured aloft, and the canvas vanished as though by magic as the ships swung round to their cables.

'Pretty fair,' said Hornblower to himself, realizing, with an inward smile at his own weakness, that no evolution could ever be carried out to his perfect satisfaction. Forward the saluting gun began to crash out its marks of respect for the Russian flag; Hornblower saw a puff of smoke from the fortress and then the sound of the first gun of the return salute reached his ears. Eleven guns; they recognized his broad pendant, then, and knew what compliments were due to a Commodore.

In these conditions of doubtful neutrality it would be best for the first contact with the shore to be made by Basse. At least ostensibly the squadron had come to Kronstadt merely to bring him with his news to the Swedish Crown Prince. Hornblower had his barge hoisted out and sent Basse away in it, and the boat returned without him but with no other information. Apart from the salute the Russian Empire chose to ignore the British squadron's existence.

'Call me if anything happens, if you please, Captain Bush,' said Hornblower.

He went off below to his cabin; Brown relieved him of his heavy full-dress coat with the epaulettes, and, once more alone, he began to fidget about the cabin. He stepped out into the stern gallery and returned to the cabin. The realization that he was worried annoyed him; he took down Archdeacon Coxe's travels from the bookshelf and set himself seriously to read the Archdeacon's intensely wearisome remarks about the condition of Russia, in the endeavour to inform himself more fully about the northern powers. But the words made sheer nonsense to him. He got up from his chair and made himself lie on his cot, shut his eyes and grimly clenched his hands and tried to force himself to doze. The minutes passed on leaden feet; he felt he had never felt so caged and unhappy before in his life.

Eight bells went, and he heard the watch relieved; it was like an eternity before he heard a bustle on the half-deck outside and someone knocked on the door. Hornblower settled himself in an attitude of complete relaxation on his cot.

'Come in!' he called, and he blinked and peered at the midshipman as if he had just awakened from a sound sleep.

'Boat heading towards us, sir,' said the midshipman.

'I'll come up,' said Hornblower. 'Pass the word for my cox'n.'

Brown helped him into his dress-coat, and he reached the deck while the boat was still some distance off.

The pinnace came into the wind, and took in her mainsail while the bowman hailed the ship in Russian.

'Where's Mr Braun?' said Hornblower.

The hail was repeated, and Braun translated.

'He is asking permission to hook on to us, sir. And he says he has a message for you.'

'Tell him to come alongside,' said Hornblower. This dependence upon an interpreter always irritated him.

The boat's crew was smart, dressed in something like a uniform with blue shirts and white trousers, and in the stern-sheets, ready to mount the side, was an officer in military uniform, frogged across the breast in Hussar fashion. The Hussar came clumsily up the side, and glanced round, saluting the mass of gold lace which awaited him. Then he produced a letter, which he offered with a further explanation in Russian.

'From His Imperial Majesty the Czar,' translated Braun with a catch in his voice.

Hornblower took the letter; it was addressed in French:

M. LE CHEF D'ESCADRE LE CAPITAINE SIR HORNBLOWER,
VAISSEAU BRITANNIQUE NOONSUCH.

Apparently the Czar's secretary, however competent he might be in other ways, was shaky regarding both British titles and spelling. The letter within was written in French as well—it was pleasant to be able to translate without Braun's assistance.

The Imperial Palace of Peterhof
Grand Marshalate of the Imperial Court
May 30th, 1812

Sir,

I am commanded by His Imperial Majesty the Emperor of All the Russias to express to you His Imperial Majesty's pleasure at hearing of your arrival in His Imperial Majesty's waters. His Imperial Majesty and His Royal Highness the Prince of Sweden further command you to dinner at this palace to-day at four o'clock accompanied by your staff. His Excellency the Minister of Marine has put at your disposal a boat which will convey you and your party direct to the quay, and the officer who conveys this letter to you will serve as your guide.

Accept, sir, the assurances of my highest consideration,
KOTCHUBEY,
Grand Marshal of the Court

'I am invited to dinner with the Czar and Bernadotte,' said Hornblower to Bush; he handed over the letter, and Bush looked at it wisely with his head on one side as if he could read French.

'You're going, I suppose, sir?'

'Yes.'

It would hardly be tactful to begin his first encounter with the Russian and Swedish authorities by refusing an Imperial and a royal command.

Hornblower suddenly became aware that the Hussar had yet another letter in his hand. He took it from him and glanced at the superscription.

'Here, Colonel, this is for you,' he said, handing it to Wychwood before turning back to Bush. 'The Czar and

Bernadotte are at Peterhof—the palace is marked on the chart, on the Oranienbaum shore over there. You will be in command in my absence, of course.'

Bush's face reflected a complexity of emotions; Hornblower knew that he was remembering other occasions when Hornblower had left him in command, to go on shore to beard a mad tyrant on the coast of Central America, or to undertake some hare-brained adventure on the coast of France.

'Aye aye, sir,' said Bush.

'I have to take my staff,' said Hornblower. 'Who do you think would care to dine with the Czar?'

'You'll need Braun, I suppose, sir?'

'I suppose so.'

Dinner with the Czar would be a notable experience for any young officer, something he would be able to yarn about for the rest of his life. Good service could be rewarded by an invitation; and at the same time some future Admiral might gain invaluable experience.

'I'll take Hurst,' decided Hornblower; there were not the makings of an Admiral in the first lieutenant, but discipline demanded that he be included in the party. 'And young Mound, if you'll signal for him. And a midshipman. Who do you suggest?'

'Somers is the brightest, sir.'

'The fat one? Very good, I'll take him. Have you been invited, too, Colonel?'

'I have, sir,' answered Wychwood.

'We must be there at four,' said Hornblower. 'We'll leave in half an hour.'

Hornblower came punctually to the ship's side to find the others awaiting him, young Somers' plump cheeks empurpled with the constriction of his stock, Hurst and Mound uncomfortable in their full dress, Braun stiffly uniformed.

'Carry on,' said Hornblower.

Young Somers went first in accordance with the age-old rule of the junior getting first into a boat, and Braun followed him. Braun's lifted arm, as he went over the side, pulled up his tight coat for a moment, and his waistcoat with it. Something flashed momentarily into view at his waistband; something black—Hornblower's eyes were resting on it at that moment. It must have been the butt of a pistol, the barrel of it pushed into the waistband of his breeches, round by his hip where the bulge would be least noticeable. The fellow was wearing his sword, of course. Hornblower began to wonder why he should take a pistol. But Mound and Hurst had followed him down by this time, and Wychwood was heaving himself over, in his scarlet tunic and bearskin. The Hussar should go next, so that the Commodore should descend last, but he was hanging back with misplaced politeness, bowing and making way for the Commodore.

'After you, sir,' said Hornblower to his deaf ears.

Hornblower had positively to stamp his foot to compel the ignorant soldier to precede him, and then he swung himself over to the shrilling of the pipes of the boatswain's mates and the rigid salutes of the ship's officers. He dropped into the sternsheets, encumbered with his boat-cloak. There was a tiny cabin forward, where he joined Wychwood and Hurst. Mound and the warrant officers and the Hussar kept themselves discreetly in the stern. The coxswain yelled some strange order and the boat cast off, the lugsail was hoisted and they headed over to the Oranienbaum shore.

From where he sat Hornblower could see Braun sitting stiffly in the sternsheets. That business of the pistol was rather curious. Presumably he had fears of attack or arrest on shore as a recent rebel, and wished to have the means to defend himself. But not even the Russians would lay hands on an English officer, in a British uniform.

The coxswain suddenly shouted a new order, and the pinnace came about on the other tack; the dipping lug with which she was equipped had to be taken in and reset when she tacked, and Hornblower watched the evolution with professional interest. The Russian sailors were smart and handy enough, but that was to be expected of the crew of the pinnace specially attached to the service of the Russian Admiralty. The *Nonsuch* was already far astern, hull down. A buoy made its appearance close alongside, and passed away astern, the rapidity of its passage proof of the speed the pinnace was making through the water.

'I know nothing about the Peterhof,' remarked Wychwood. 'I was in Czarskoe Selo and the old Winter Palace as a subaltern on Wilson's staff before Tilsit. The Peterhof's one of the lesser palaces; I expect they chose it for this meeting so that Bernadotte could arrive direct by sea.'

It was quite futile to debate what would be the result of this evening's meeting, and yet the temptation was overwhelming. The minutes slipped by until the coxswain shouted a new order. The lugsail came down, and the piles of a jetty came into sight beside the pinnace as she rounded-to. Lines were thrown out and the pinnace drew in beside a broad companionway run down into the water from the top of the jetty. Hornblower ducked out of the little cabin, stepped on to the companionway and began to walk up, hurriedly making sure that his cocked hat was on straight and his sword properly slung. As he reached the top someone shouted an order; there was a guard of twenty soldiers drawn up there, grenadiers in bearskins and blue coats. They put their left arms across their breasts as they presented arms in a fashion that appeared back-handed to a man accustomed to receiving salutes from

the Royal Marines. Hornblower stiffly returned the salute
of the officer of the guard, standing at attention long enough
for the rest of the party to catch him up; the Hussar spoke
rapidly to Braun in Russian.

'There are carriages waiting for us, sir,' Braun interpreted.

Hornblower could see them at the end of the jetty, two big
open laudaus, with fine horses to each; in the drivers' seats
sat coachmen pigtailed and powdered wearing red coats—
not the scarlet of the British Army or of the British royal
liveries, but a softer, strawberry red. Footmen similarly
dressed stood at the horses' heads and at the carriage doors.

'Senior officers go in the first carriage,' explained Braun.

Hornblower climbed in, with Wychwood and Hurst after
him; with an apologetic smile the Hussar followed them and
sat with his back to the horses. The door shut. One footman
leaped up beside the coachman and the other sprang up
behind, and the horses dashed forward. The road wound
through a vast park, alternate sweeps of grass and groves of
trees; here and there fountains threw lofty jets of water at the
sky, and marble naiads posed by marble basins. Occasional
turns in the road opened up beautiful vistas down the terraced
lawns; there were long flights of marble steps and beautiful
little marble pavilions, but also, at every turning, beside every
fountain and every pavilion, there were sentries on guard,
stiffly presenting arms as the carriages whirled by.

'Every Czar for the last three generations has been
murdered,' remarked Wychwood. 'It's only the women who
die in their beds. Alexander is taking precautions.'

The carriage turned sharply again and came out on a broad
gravelled parade ground; on the farther side Hornblower
just had time to see the palace, a rambling rococo building
of pink and grey stone with a dome at either end, before the
carriage drew up at the entrance to the salute of a further

guard, and a white-powdered footman opened the doors. With a few polite words in Russian the Hussar led the party forward up a flight of pink marble steps and into a lofty ante-room. A swarm of servants came forward to take their boat-cloaks; Hornblower remembered to put his cocked hat under his arm and the others followed his example. The folding doors beyond were thrown open, and they went towards them, to be received by a dignified official whose coat was of the same Imperial red where the colour was visible through the gold lace. He wore powder and carried in his hand a gold-tipped ebony stave.

'Kotchubey,' he said, speaking fair French. 'Grand Marshal of the Palace. Commodore Hornblower? Lord Wychwood?'

They bowed to him, and Hornblower presented the others; he saw the Grand Marshal run an all-embracing eye over their uniforms to make sure that nothing unworthy of the Court of the Czar would penetrate farther into the palace. Then he turned back to Hornblower and Wychwood.

'His Excellency the Minister of Marine would be honoured if Commodore Hornblower would grant him time for a short interview.'

'I am at His Excellency's service,' said Hornblower, 'but I am here at the command of His Imperial Majesty.'

'That is very good of you, sir. There will be time before His Imperial Majesty appears. And His Excellency the Minister of Foreign Affairs would be honoured by Lord Wychwood's attention for a few minutes in a similar way.'

'I am at His Excellency's service,' said Wychwood. For a man of his experience his French was remarkably poor.

'Thank you,' said Kotchubey.

He turned, and three more officers of the Court approached at his gesture. They wore less gold lace than Kotchubey, and from the gold keys embroidered on their lapels Hornblower

knew them to be chamberlains. There were further introductions, more bows.

'Now if you have the kindness to accompany me, sir——'
said Kotchubey to Hornblower.

Two chamberlains took charge of the junior officers, one
took charge of Wychwood, and Kotchubey led Hornblower
away. Hornblower gave one last glance at his party. Even
the stolid Hurst, even the deliberately languid Mound, wore
rather scared expressions at being abandoned by their captain
like this in an Imperial palace. But Braun's expression was
different. His green eyes were glowing with excitement, and
there was a new tenseness about his features, and he was
casting glances about him like a man preparing himself for
some decisive action. Hornblower felt a wave of misgiving
break over him; during the excitement of setting foot in
Russia he had forgotten about Braun, about the pistol, about
everything connected with him. He wanted time to think, and
yet Kotchubey was hurrying him away and allowing him no
time. They walked through a magnificent room—Hornblower
was only just conscious of its furniture, pictures, and statuary
—and through folding doors beyond, which were opened for
them by two of the footmen who seemed to be present in
hundreds. The corridor was wide and lofty, more like a
picture gallery than a corridor, but Kotchubey only went a
few yards along it. He stopped abruptly at an inconspicuous
door, from before which two more footmen stepped with
alacrity at his approach. The door opened straight upon a
steep winding stairway; half-way up there was another door,
this one guarded by four burly soldiers in pink uniforms with
high boots and baggy breeches whom Hornblower recognized
as the first Cossacks he had ever seen in the flesh. They nearly
jammed the narrow stairway as they drew back against the
wall to make way; Hornblower had to push past them.

Kotchubey scratched upon the door and instantly opened it, immediately drawing Hornblower after him with a gesture as though he were a conspirator.

'Sir Hornblower,' he announced, having shut the door. The big man in the vaguely naval uniform, with epaulettes and a string of orders across his breast, must be the Minister of Marine; he came forward cordially, speaking fair French and with a courtly apology for not speaking English. But in the far corner of the room was another figure, tall and slender, in a beautiful light-blue uniform. He was strikingly handsome, but as though he came from another world; the ivory pallor of his cheeks, accentuated by his short black sidewhiskers, was more unnatural than unhealthy. He made no move as he sat stiffly upright in the dark corner, his finger-tips resting on a low table before him, and neither of the Russian officials gave any overt sign of acknowledging his presence, but Hornblower knew that it was the Czar; thinking quickly, he realized that if the Czar's own officials pretended the Czar was not there, then he could do no less. He kept his eyes on the Minister of Marine's.

'I trust,' said the latter, 'that I see you in good health?'

'Thank you,' said Hornblower. 'I am in the best of health.'

'And your squadron?'

'That is in the best of health too, Your Excellency.'

'Does it need anything?'

Hornblower had to think quickly again. On the one hand was the desire to appear utterly independent, but on the other there was the nagging knowledge that water would soon be running short. Every commanding officer, whether of ships or squadron, carried always at the back of his mind the vital, urgent need for renewing his ship's drinking water. And a Minister of Marine—even a Russian one—must be aware of that.

'Firewood and water, as always,' said Hornblower, 'would be of the greatest convenience.'

'I shall inquire if it is convenient to send a water-boat to your squadron to-morrow morning,' said the Minister.

'I thank Your Excellency,' said Hornblower, wondering what he would be asked to do in exchange.

'You have been informed, sir,' said the Minister, changing the subject so obviously that Hornblower could only attribute it to nervousness at having the Czar listening to the conversation, 'of Bonaparte's occupation of Swedish Pomerania?'

'Yes, Your Excellency.'

'And what is your opinion of that transaction?'

Hornblower delayed his answer while he sorted out his thoughts and worked out the French phrases.

'Typical Bonapartism,' he said. 'He tolerates neutrality on the part of weak powers only while he can profit by it. The moment he finds it inconveniences him, he treacherously sends forward his army, and on the heels of the army march all the plagues of Bonapartism, terror and famine and misery. The gaol, the firing party, and the secret police. The bankers and the merchants are stripped of all they possess. The men are thrust into the ranks of his army, and the women—all the world knows what happens to the women.'

'But do you not believe his object was merely plunder?'

'No, Your Excellency—although plunder is always useful to Bonaparte's top-heavy finances. He overran Pomerania the moment it was apparent that its usefulness as a neutral base for his privateers had ceased with the appearance of my squadron.'

Inspiration came to Hornblower at that moment; his expression must have changed, for as he hesitated the Minister prompted him with obvious interest.

'Monsieur was going to say——?'

'Bonaparte controls the whole Baltic coast now as far as the frontiers of His Imperial Majesty's dominions. That would be most convenient to him in one particular event, Your Excellency. In the event of his deciding to launch an attack on Russia.' Hornblower threw into those words all the power of speech that he could muster, and the Minister nodded—Hornblower did not dare, much as he wanted to, to throw a glance at the Czar to see what effect his words had on him.

'Bonaparte would never feel easy in his mind regarding his communications while Pomerania was Swedish so long as there was a British fleet in the Baltic. It could be too good a base for an attack on his rear, convoyed by my squadron. He has eliminated that danger now—he can march an army against St Petersburg, should he attack Russia, without fear of its being cut off. It is one more threat to His Imperial Majesty's dominions.'

'And how serious do you consider his threats to be regarding Russia, sir?'

'Bonaparte's threats are always serious. You know his methods, Your Excellency. A demand for concessions, and when the concessions are granted then new demands, each one more weakening than the one before, until either the object of his attentions is too weak to oppose him further or is at least so weakened as to make armed resistance fatal. He will not rest until all his demands are granted; and what he demands is nothing short of the dominion of the world, until every nation is in bondage to him.'

'Monsieur is very eloquent.'

'I am eloquent because I speak from the heart, Your Excellency. For nineteen years, since my boyhood, I have served my country against the monstrous power which overshadows Europe.'

'And with what effect has your country fought?'

'My country is still free. In the history of the world that counts for much. And now it counts for more. England is striking back. Portugal, Sicily, are free too, thanks to England. Her armies are marching into Spain even while I am speaking to you here, Your Excellency. Soon Bonaparte will be defending the very frontiers of his boasted Empire against them. We have found the weak spot in the vast structure; we are probing into it, on to the very foundations, and soon the whole elaborate mass will crumble into ruin.'

The little room must be very warm; Hornblower found himself sweating in his heavy uniform.

'And here in the Baltic?'

'Here England has penetrated too. Not one of Bonaparte's ships will move from to-day without my permission. England is ready with her support. She is ready to pour in money and arms to help any power that will withstand the tyrant. Bonaparte is ringed in from the South and the West and the North. There is only the East left to him. That is where he will strike and that is where he must be opposed.'

It was the handsome, pale young man in the dark corner of the room to whom these remarks were really addressed. The Minister of Marine had a far smaller stake on the board of international politics than did his master. Other kings in war risked a province or two, risked their dignity or their fame, but the Czar of Russia, the most powerful and autocratic of them all, risked his life, and there was no gainsaying that. A word from the Czar might send a nobleman to Siberia; another word might set half a million men on the move to war; but if either move were a false one the Czar would pay for it with his life. A military defeat, a momentary loss of control over his courtiers or his guards, and the Czar was doomed, first to dethronement and then to inevitable murder. That had been the fate of his father, of his grand-father, and of his great-grandfather. If he fought and was unsuccessful; if he did not fight and lost his prestige there would be a silken scarf round his throat or a dozen swords between his ribs.

An ormulu clock on a bracket on the wall struck in silvery tones.

'The hour strikes, you see, Your Excellency,' said Horn-blower. He was shaking with the excitement that boiled within him. He felt weak and empty.

'The hour strikes indeed,' answered the Minister. He was clearly struggling desperately not to glance back at the Czar. 'As regards the clock, I regret it deeply, as it reminds me that if I detain you longer you will be late for the Imperial reception.'

'I must certainly not be late for that,' said Hornblower.

'I must thank you for the clear way in which you have stated your views, Captain. I shall have the pleasure of meeting you at the reception. His Excellency the Grand Marshal will show you the way to the Tauride Hall.'

Hornblower bowed, still keeping his eyes from wavering towards the Czar, but he contrived to back from the room without either turning his back on the Czar or making his precaution too obvious. They squeezed past the Cossacks on the stairs down to the ground floor again.

'This way, if you please, sir.'

An Attempt at Assassination

FOOTMEN opened two more huge doors, and they entered a vast room, the lofty ceiling soaring into a dome far above their heads. The walls were a mass of marble and gold, and grouped in the hall was a crowd of people, the men in uniforms of all the colours of the rainbow, the women in Court dresses with plumes and trains. Orders and jewels reflected the light of innumerable candles.

A group of men and women, laughing and joking in French, opened their ranks to admit Hornblower and the Grand Marshal.

'I have the honour to present——' began the latter. It was a prolonged introduction; the Countess of This, and the Baroness of That, and the Duchess of the Other, beautiful women, some of them bold-eyed and some of them languid. Hornblower bowed and bowed again, the Star of the Bath thumping his chest each time he straightened up.

'You will partner the Countess Canerine at dinner, Captain,' said the Grand Marshal, and Hornblower bowed again.

'Delighted,' he said.

The Countess was the boldest-eyed and most beautiful of them all; under the arches of her brows her eyes were dark and liquid and yet with a consuming fire within them.

'As a distinguished stranger,' went on the Grand Marshal, 'you will take precedence immediately after the Ambassadors and Ministers. Preceding you will be the Persian Ambassador, His Excellency Gorza Khan.'

The Grand Marshal indicated an individual in turban and diamonds; it was a bit of blessed good fortune that he was the most easily identified person in the whole crowd.

Hornblower caught sight of Wychwood across the room, his bearskin under his arm and Basse at his side, being introduced to another group. They exchanged nods, and Hornblower returned, a little distractedly, to the conversation of his own group. The Countess was asking him about his ship, and he tried to tell her about *Nonsuch*. Through the far doors there was filing a double line of soldiers, tall young men in breast-plates that shone like silver—that probably were silver—with silver helmets with waving white plumes.

'The Chevalier Guard,' exclaimed the Countess, 'all young men of noble birth.'

She looked at them with distinct approval; they were form-ing against the walls at intervals of two or three yards, each standing like a silver statue as soon as he reached his post. The crowd was moving slowly away from the centre of the room, leaving it clear. Hornblower wondered where the rest of his officers were; he looked round, and realized that there was a further crowd of uniformed individuals in the gallery which ran at first-floor level three-quarters of the way round the dome over his head. That would be where the lesser people could look down on the doings of the great. He saw Hurst and Mound leaning against the balustrade. Behind them young Somers, his low-crowned hat in his hand, was talking with elaborate pantomime to a trio of pretty girls, who were holding weakly on to each other as they laughed. Heaven only knew what language Somers was trying to talk, but he was evidently making himself agreeable.

It was Braun that Hornblower was worried about; yet

what with the violence of his reaction after his speech-making, and the chatter and glitter around him, it was hard to think. Hornblower had to drive himself to keep his mind on his subject. The pistol in Braun's waistband—the fierce intensity of Braun's expression—that gallery up there. He could fit the pieces of the puzzle together if only he were left undistracted for a moment.

'The Prince of Sweden will make his entry with His Imperial Majesty,' the Countess was saying.

The Prince of Sweden! Bernadotte, the initiator of a new dynasty, the supplanter of Gustavus, for whom Braun had risked life and fortune. Alexander had conquered Finland; Bernadotte had abandoned it to him. The two men whom Braun had most reason to hate in the whole world were probably Alexander and Bernadotte. And Braun was armed with a double-barrelled pistol. Hornblower swept the gallery with his eyes. There he was, at the far end, standing unobtrusively between two pillars. Something must be done at once. The Grand Marshal was chattering affably with a couple of courtiers, and Hornblower turned to him, abandoning the Countess and breaking rudely into the conversation with the only excuse that he could think of.

'Impossible!' said the Grand Marshal, glancing at the clock. 'His Imperial Majesty and His Royal Highness enter in three and a half minutes.'

'I'm sorry,' said Hornblower. 'I regret it deeply, but I must—it is absolutely necessary—it is urgent——'

Hornblower fairly danced with anxiety, and the gesture reinforced the argument he had already advanced. The Grand Marshal stood weighing the relative undesirability of interrupting a Court ceremony and offending someone who, as the recent interview showed, might have the ear of the Czar.

'Go out through that door, then, sir,' he said reluctantly at length, pointing, 'and please, sir, come back without calling attention to yourself.'

Hornblower fled, sidling rapidly but as unobtrusively as possible through the groups of people to the door; he slipped through it and glanced round desperately. The broad staircase to the left must lead up to the gallery. He grasped the scabbard of his sword to keep it from tripping him up and ran up the stairs two at a time; the one or two footmen whom he passed hardly spared him a glance. The gallery was crowded, although the dresses were not as beautiful nor the uniforms as brilliant. Hornblower hurried along towards the end where he had seen Braun; he took long strides while doing his best to look like a nonchalant stroller. Mound caught his eye— Hornblower could not spare the time to say anything, dared not risk saying a word, but he put all the meaning into his glance that he could, hoping that Mound would follow him. Down below he heard the sound of doors being thrown open, and the babble of conversation stopped abruptly. A loud harsh voice announced 'L'Empéreur! L'Impératrice! Le Prince Royal de Suède!'

Braun stood there between the two pillars, glancing down. His hand was at his waist; he was drawing the pistol. There was only one silent way to stop him. Hornblower whipped out his sword and slashed at the wrist of the hand that held the pistol. With the tendons severed the fingers opened nervelessly and the pistol fell heavily on the carpeted floor while Braun turned in gaping surprise, looking first at the blood spouting from his wrist and then at Hornblower's face. Hornblower put the point of the blade at his breast; he could lunge and kill him on the instant, and every line in his expression must have attested the genuineness of his determination to do so if necessary, for Braun uttered no sound, made no

There was only one silent way to stop him

movement. Somebody loomed up at Hornblower's shoulder; it was Mound, thank God.

'Look after him,' whispered Hornblower. 'Tie that wrist up! Get him out of here somehow.'

He glanced over the railing. A little crowd of royalty was advancing through the huge doors opposite and below him— Alexander in his light-blue uniform; a tall swarthy man with a huge nose who must be Bernadotte; a number of women, two with crowns who must be the Empress and Empress-Mother, and the rest in plumes. Braun would have had the easiest shot heart could desire. All round the vast room the Court was making obeisance, the men bowing low and the woman curtseying; as Hornblower looked they rose all together, plumes and uniforms like a breaking wave of flowers. Hornblower tore his eyes from the spectacle, sheathed his sword, and picked up the pistol from the floor, stuffing it down into his waistband. Mound, his eternal nonchalance replaced by swift cat-like movements, had his long arms round Braun, who was leaning against him. Hornblower snatched out his handkerchief and put it in Mound's hand, but there was not time to do more. He turned away and hastened back along the gallery. The lesser courtiers up here had straightened up from their bows and their curtseys and were beginning to look around them again and resume their conversation. It was lucky that at the moment of crisis they had had no eyes or ears for anything save the royal party. Hurst and Somers were about to start talking to the women again when Hornblower caught their eyes.

'Go back there to Mound,' he said. 'He needs your help.'

Then he walked quickly down the stairs again, found the door into the audience hall, and pushed past the footman on guard there. A glance showed him the position of the group he had left, and he sidled round to it and took up his position at the Countess's side. The royal party was making the circle of the room, making the usual conventional remarks to distinguished individuals, and it was only a matter of a few minutes before they reached Hornblower. The Grand Marshal presented him, and Hornblower, his head swimming with his recent excitement so that he felt as if he was in a nightmare, bowed to each crowned head in turn and to Bernadotte.

'It is a pleasure to meet Commodore Hornblower,' said Alexander pleasantly. 'We have all of us heard of his exploits.'

'Your Majesty is too kind,' gulped Hornblower.

Then the royal group passed on, and Hornblower turned to meet the Countess's glance again. The fact that the Czar had addressed a few words to him personally evidently confirmed her suspicions that he was a man of potential influence, and there was a considering look in her eyes.

'Will you be making a long stay in Russia?' she asked.

It was very hard, during this period of intense reaction, to keep his mind on anything. All he wanted to do was to sit down and rest quietly. He flogged his mind into making a polite rejoinder, and when the men of the party began to ply him with questions about the British Navy and about maritime affairs in general he tried to answer sensibly, but it was a forlorn hope.

Footmen were rolling in long buffet tables, glittering with gold and silver; Hornblower forced himself to watch keenly, so as to commit no breach of etiquette. To one side the royal party had taken their seats, Empresses and Czar in armchairs and the princes and princesses in upright chairs, and everyone had to be careful always to face in that direction so as not to commit the heinous crime of letting royalty see a human back.

People were beginning to take food from the buffets, and, try as he would, Hornblower could see no sign at all of any attention to precedence. But there was the Persian Ambassador munching something from a gold plate, so that he was justified in making a move in the same direction. Yet all the same this was the most curious dinner he had ever attended, with everyone standing up except royalty; and royalty, he could see, were eating nothing at all.

'May I offer you my arm, Countess?' he said, as the group began to drift towards a buffet.

The courtiers by dint of long practice had seemingly mastered the art of eating while standing up and while holding their hats under their arms, but it was not easy. His dangling sword was liable to trip him, too, and that infernal pistol in his waistband was digging uncomfortably into his side. The footmen serving at the buffets understood no French, and the Countess came to Hornblower's rescue with an order.

'That is caviare,' she explained to him, 'and this is vodka, the drink of the people, but I think you will find that the two are admirably suited to each other.'

The Countess was right. The grey, unappetizing-looking stuff was perfectly delicious. Hornblower sipped cautiously at the vodka, and in his present highly strung condition hardly noticed the fierce bite of the liquor; but there was no doubt that vodka and caviare blended together exquisitely. He felt the warm glow of the alcohol inside him, and realized that he was desperately hungry. The buffet was covered with foods of all kinds, some being kept warm in chafing dishes, some cold; under the tutelage of the Countess, Hornblower went a fair way towards tackling them all. It might be a queer way to have dinner, but Hornblower thought he had never tasted such delicious food. Laughter, chatter, and bright lights; this was one of the jolliest parties he had ever attended —he felt as if it had been someone else who had slashed Braun's wrist open with a sword an hour ago. He was comfortably replete, with the gratifying sensation of having eaten just too much and having drunk just enough; he supposed coffee would be served soon, and a cup of coffee was all he needed to complete his internal gratification.

'I have dined extremely well,' he said to the Countess.

The most remarkable expression passed over the Countess's face. Her eyebrows rose, and she opened her mouth to say something and then shut it again. She was smiling and puzzled and distressed all at the same time. She again started to speak, but her words were cut short by the ceremonial opening of yet another pair of doors from which twenty or thirty footmen emerged to form an avenue leading into the next room. Hornblower became conscious that the royal party had risen from their chairs and were falling into formation, and the complete cessation of conversation told Hornblower that some specially solemn moment had arrived. Couples were moving about the room like ships jockeying for position. The Countess laid her hand on his arm with a gentle pressure as if to lead him. By George, a procession was forming behind the royal party! There went the Persian Ambassador, a smiling girl on his arm. Hornblower just had time to lead his own partner forward to join the procession next, and after two or three more couples had joined behind him the procession began to move forward, its tail being steadily lengthened as it went. Hornblower kept his eyes on the Persian Ambassador before him; they passed down the avenue of footmen, and entered the next room.

The procession was breaking off to left and to right in alternate couples as though in a country dance; the Persian Ambassador went to the left, and Hornblower was ready to go to the right without the prompting of the gesture of the Grand Marshal, who was standing there ready to direct anyone in doubt. It was another enormous room, lit by what seemed to be hundreds of cut-glass chandeliers dangling from the roof, and all down the length of it ran a vast table covered with gold plate and crystal and embanked with flowers. The table was shaped like a T with a very small crosspiece, and the royal party had already taken their seats at the head; behind every chair all the way down stood a white-wigged footman. It dawned upon Hornblower that dinner was about to begin; the food and drink which had been served in the domed hall had been something extra and introductory. Hornblower was ready to laugh at himself for his idiotic lack of comprehension at the same time as he was ready to groan with despair at the thought of having to eat his way through an Imperial dinner in his present distended condition.

Save for royalty, the men were standing at their chairs while the ladies sat; across the table the Persian Ambassador was bending affably over the young woman he had brought in, and the aigrette in his turban nodded and his diamonds flashed. The last woman took her seat, and then the men sat down together—not quite as simultaneously as marines presenting arms, but almost so. A babble of conversation began immediately, and almost immediately a golden soup plate was put under Hornblower's nose and a golden soup tureen full of pink soup was offered to him for him to help himself from. He could not help glancing down the table; everyone had been given soup at the same moment—there must be two hundred footmen at least waiting at table.

'That is M. de Narbonne, the French Ambassador,' said the Countess, indicating with a glance a handsome young man across the table two places higher than the Persian Ambassador. 'Of course the Grand Marshal did not present you to him. And that is the Austrian Ambassador, and the Saxon Minister, and the Danish Minister, all your enemies officially. The Spanish Ambassador comes from Joseph Bonaparte, not from the Spanish partisan government which you recognize, so you could hardly be presented to him either. I don't believe there's a soul here except us Russians to whom it would be proper to present you.'

There was a cool, pleasant yellow wine in a tall glass before Hornblower, and he sipped it. The golden soup plate was whisked away and replaced by a golden dinner plate. His footman spoke to him in Russian, apparently offering him a choice, and the Countess settled the problem without referring to him.

'As this is your first visit to Russia,' she explained, 'I could be sure that you have not yet tasted our Volga River trout.'

She was helping herself to one as she spoke, from a golden dish; Hornblower's footman was presenting another golden dish.

'A gold service looks very well,' said the Countess sadly, 'but it allows the food to grow unfortunately cold. I never use mine in my house save when I entertain His Imperial Majesty. As that is the case in most houses I doubt if His Imperial Majesty ever has a hot meal.'

A couple of fat little birds on toast followed the trout; they melted delicately in the mouth; some other wine followed the champagne. And there was a venison stew, and a cut of some roast which might be mutton but which was borne on Pegasus-wings of garlic beyond mundane speculation. Somewhere in the procession of food appeared a pink water ice, only the third or fourth which Hornblower had ever tasted.

They were drinking toasts at the head of the table—for the first one everyone had to stand while they drank the health of the Prince of Sweden, and after that conversation perforce became disjointed with other toasts to be drunk, announced by a gigantic official with a colossal voice—Stentor with Hercules' frame, said Hornblower to himself, pleased with the classical touch—who stood behind the Czar's chair. Between toasts there was music; not orchestral music, but vocal music from an unaccompanied male choir, seemingly of hundreds of voices which filled the vast room with their din. It was a relief when the music ceased and everyone stood once more while the royal party withdrew through a doorway near the head of the table, and no sooner had the door closed after them than the women went out too, ushered through the far door by Madame Kotchubey.

The men began to gather in groups along the table while footmen hastened in with coffee and cordials; Wychwood, his bearskin still under his arm, made his way round to Hornblower. His face was redder than ever; his eyes, if it were possible, stuck out even farther from his head.

'The Swedes'll fight if Russia will,' said Wychwood, in a grating whisper, 'I have that direct from Basse, who was with Bernadotte all day.'

Then he passed on and Hornblower heard his remarkable French being practised on a uniformed group higher up the table. The room was unbearably hot, presumably because of the infinity of candles alight in it; some of the men were already beginning to drift away through the door where the women had preceded them. Hornblower drank his coffee and rose to his feet, transferring his cocked hat once more from his knees to under his arm. The room he entered must have been the counterpart of the one in which the royal reception had been held, for it was domed too, and of similar proportions; Hornblower remembered the two domes he had seen when his carriage drew up to the palace.

From the number of people already assembled it was clear that this was the meeting-place of the whole Court; presumably the hundreds of people who had perforce witnessed the royal reception from the gallery were permitted to descend and mingle with their betters after dining less elaborately. Young Mound was lounging towards him, his lean gangling body looking like an overgrown colt's.

'We have him in a side room aloft, sir,' he reported. 'He fainted with the loss of blood—we had to put a tourniquet on his arm to stop the bleeding. We bandaged him with half of Somers' shirt, and Somers and Mr Hurst are keeping guard over him.'

'Does anyone know about it?'

'No, sir. We got him into the room without anyone seeing us. I poured a glass of liquor over his coat and from the stink of him anyone'll think he's drunk.'

Mound was obviously a capable man in an emergency, as Hornblower had already suspected.

'Very good.'

'The sooner we get him away the better, sir,' said Mound, with a diffidence to be expected of a junior officer making suggestions to a senior.

'You're quite right,' said Hornblower, 'except that——'

Hornblower was still having to think quickly. It would hardly be possible, in any case, to leave at once, the moment dinner was over. It would not be polite. They simply could not leave immediately.

'We shall have to stay another hour at least,' he said. 'The conventions demand it. Go back and hold the fort for that time.'

'Aye aye, sir.'

Mound restrained himself in the nick of time from coming to attention as with the habit of years he had grown accustomed to do when uttering those words—further proof of the clearness of his head. He nodded and wandered off as if they had been merely discussing the weather.

A Visit
from the 'Comte du Nord'

HORNBLOWER turned over in his cot with a groan; the effort of turning brought back the pain into his temples, although he moved very cautiously. He was a fool to have drunk so much—it was the first time he had had this sort of headache for half a dozen years.

His shower-bath restored some of Hornblower's peace of mind. He put on clean linen and went up on deck, where the first person on whom he laid eyes was Wychwood, bleary-eyed and obviously with a far worse headache than he had himself. Yet the keen air of the Russian morning was invigorating and refreshing. The normal early-morning ship's routine, the sight of the rows of men holystoning the decks, the pleasant swish of the water over the planking, were comforting and restorative as well.

'Boat coming off to us, sir,' reported a midshipman to the officer of the watch.

It was the same pinnace as had taken them ashore yesterday, and it brought a naval officer with a letter in French:

His Excellency the Minister of the Imperial Marine presents his compliments to Commodore Sir Hornblower. His Excellency has given orders for a water-boat to be alongside the Nonsuch *at eleven o'clock this morning.*

A distinguished nobleman, M. le Comte du Nord, having expressed a desire to see one of His Britannic Majesty's Ships, His Excellency proposes to trespass upon Sir Hornblower's hospitality by visiting the Nonsuch *at ten o'clock in company with the Comte du Nord.*

Hornblower showed the letter to Wychwood, who confirmed his suspicions.

'That's Alexander,' he said. 'He used the title of Comte du Nord when he was travelling on the continent as Czarevitch. He'll be coming incognito, so that there'll be no need for royal honours.'

Bush heard the news with a low whistle, and instantly turned to sweep decks and rigging with his glance, anxious that his ship should be in the perfection of condition for this Imperial visit.

'How can we take in water,' asked Bush piteously, 'and be in a fit state for the Czar to come on board, sir? What will he think of us? Unless we water the flotilla first.'

'The Czar's a man of sense,' said Hornblower, briskly. 'Let's show him the hands at work. He doesn't know the difference between the mizzen-stay and the flying jib-boom, but he'll recognize efficient work if we show it to him. Start watering while he's on board.'

'And the food?' asked Bush. 'We'll have to offer him something, sir.'

Hornblower grinned at his anxiety.

'Yes, we'll offer him something.'

It was typical of Hornblower's contrary temperament that the more difficulties other people foresaw the more cheerful he became; the only person really capable of depressing Hornblower was Hornblower himself. His headache had left him completely, and he was positively smiling now at the thought of a busy morning. He ate his breakfast with appetite, and put on his full-dress uniform once more and came on deck to find Bush still fussing round the ship, with the crew all in clean white frocks and duck trousers, the accommodation ladder rigged, with hand-ropes as white as snow, the marines all pipeclayed and polished, the hammocks stowed in mathematical tiers. It was only when the midshipman of the watch reported a cutter approaching that he felt a little twinge of nervousness, a sudden catch in his breath, at the thought that the next few hours might have a decided bearing on the history of the world for years to come.

The calls of the boatswain's mates shrilled through the ship, and the ship's company fell in by divisions, officers to the front with epaulettes and swords, and Hornblower at the quarter-deck rail looked down at the assembly.

'Man the yards!' ordered Bush.

Another squeal from the pipes, and the topmen poured up the rigging in an orderly upward torrent, without a break in their speed as they hung back-downward from the futtock-shrouds, going hand-over-hand up the topgallant-shrouds like the trained gymnasts they were, running out along the yards like tight-rope walkers, each man taking up his position on the foot-ropes the moment he reached it.

The boatswain, looking with one eye over the starboard rail, gave an infinitesimal jerk of his head. A little procession of officers was coming up the accommodation ladder. The boatswain's mates put their calls to their lips. The sergeant-drummer of marines contrived to snap his fingers beside the seams of his trousers as he stood at attention, and the six side-drums roared out in a bold ruffle.

'Present arms!' bellowed Captain Norman, and the fifty muskets with fixed bayonets of the marines left the fifty

scarlet shoulders and came down vertically in front of
fifty rows of gleaming buttons, while the swords of the three
marine officers swept in the graceful arc of the military salute.

Alexander, followed by two aides-de-camp, came slowly
on board side by side with the Minister of Marine to whom
nominally all this ceremony was dedicated. He put his hand
to his hat-brim while the pipes died away in a final squeal,
the drums completed their fourth ruffle, the first gun of the
salute banged out forward, and the fifes and drums of the
marine band burst into 'Heart of Oak.' Hornblower walked
forward and saluted.

'Good morning, Commodore,' said the Minister of Marine.
'Permit me to present you to the Comte du Nord.'

Hornblower saluted again, his face as expressionless as

he could manage it even while he fought down a smile at Alexander's queer liking to be incognito.

'Good morning, Commodore,' said Alexander; with a shock Hornblower realized that he was speaking English of a sort. 'I hope our little visit does not discommode you too much?'

'Not in any way to compare with the honour done to the ship, sir,' said Hornblower, wondering as he said it whether 'sir' was the right way to address a Czar incognito. Apparently it sufficed.

'You may present your officers,' said Alexander.

Hornblower brought them up one by one, and they saluted and bowed with the uneasy stiffness to be expected of junior officers in the presence of a Czar of all the Russias, and an incognito one at that.

'I think you can give orders to prepare the ship for watering now, Captain,' said Hornblower to Bush, and then he turned back to Alexander. 'Would you care to see more of the ship, sir?'

'I would indeed,' said Alexander.

He was a very tall man, an inch or two taller than Hornblower, and he bent himself nearly double as he crouched under the low deck beams below decks and peered about with short-sighted eyes. Hornblower took him forward along the lower gun-deck, where the head clearance was no more than five feet six inches; he showed him the midshipmen's berth, and the warrant officers' mess, all the unlovely details of the life of a sailor. He called away a group of seamen, had them unstow and sling their hammocks, and get into them, so that Alexander could see more clearly what twenty-two inches per man really meant, and he gave a graphic description of a whole deck full of hammocks swinging together in a storm, with the men packed in a solid mass. They peered down through the hatchway to see the working party down there breaking out the water casks and preparing the tiers for refilling, and a whiff of the stench of the orlop came up to them—bilgewater and cheese and humanity intermingled.

'You are an officer of long service, I believe, Commodore?' said Alexander.

'Nineteen years, sir,' said Hornblower.

'And how much of that time have you spent at sea?'

'Sixteen years, sir. For nine months I was a prisoner in Spain, and for six months in France.'

'I know of your escape from France. You went through much peril to return to this life.'

Alexander's handsome forehead was wrinkled as he puzzled over the fact that a man could spend sixteen years of his life living in these conditions and still be sane and healthy.

'How long have you held your present rank?'

'As Commodore, sir, only two months. But I have nine years' seniority as Captain.'

'And before that?'

'I was six years lieutenant, and four years midshipman.'

'Four years? You lived four years in a place like the midshipmen's berth you showed me?'

'Not quite as comfortable as that, sir. I was in a frigate nearly all the time, under Sir Edward Pellew. A battleship is not quite as crowded as a frigate, sir.'

By the time they came on deck again the water-boat was already alongside. Some of the *Nonsuch's* hands were down on her decks, mingling with the Russians to help with the work. Working parties were swinging away lustily at the pumps, and the long snake-like canvas hoses pulsated at each stroke. Forward they were swaying up bundles of firewood, the men chanting as they hauled.

'Thanks to your generosity, sir,' said Hornblower, 'we will be able to keep the sea for four months if necessary without entering port.

Luncheon was served in Hornblower's cabin to a party of eight, Hornblower, Bush, the two senior lieutenants, and the four Russians. Bush was sweating with nervousness at the sight of the inhospitable table; at the last moment he had drawn Hornblower aside and pleaded unavailingly for Hornblower to change his mind and serve some of his remaining cabin delicacies as well as the plain ship's fare. Bush could not get out of his mind the obsession that it was necessary to feed the Czar well.

The Czar looked with interest at the battered pewter tureen which Brown set before Hornblower.

'Pea soup, sir,' explained Hornblower. 'One of the great delicacies of shipboard life.'

Carlin, of long habit, began to rap his biscuit on the table, stopped when he realized what he was doing, and then started rapping again, guiltily. He remembered the orders Hornblower had given, that everyone should behave as if no distinguished company were present. Alexander looked at Carlin and then inquiringly at Bush beside him.

'Mr Carlin is knocking out the weevils, sir,' explained Bush, almost overcome with self-consciousness. 'If you tap gently they come out of their own accord, this way, you see, sir.'

'Very interesting,' said Alexander, but he ate no bread; one of his aides-de-camp repeated the experiment, peered down at the fat white weevils with black heads that emerged, and exploded into what must have been a string of Russian oaths—almost the first words he had said since boarding the ship.

The visitors, after this inauspicious beginning, gingerly

tasted the soup. But in the British Navy pea soup, as Horn-blower had remarked, was the best dish served; the aide-de-camp who had sworn at the weevils exclaimed with surprised gratification when he had tasted it, speedily consumed his plateful, and accepted another. There were only three dishes served as the next course, boiled salt ribs of beef, boiled salt-beef tongue, and boiled salt pork, with pickled cabbage to accompany the meat. Alexander studied the three dishes, and wisely accepted the tongue; the Minister of Marine and the aides-de-camp, at Hornblower's suggestion, took a mixed plateful, carved for them by Hornblower and Bush and Hurst.

Brown was now serving rum.

'The life-blood of the Navy, sir,' said Hornblower, as Alexander studied his tumbler. 'May I offer you gentlemen a toast which we can all drink with the heartiest goodwill? The Emperor of All the Russias! Vive l'Empereur!'

All rose except Alexander to drink the toast, and they were hardly seated before Alexander was on his feet in turn.

'Commodore Sir Horatio Hornblower, and the British Royal Navy.'

As the glasses were drained, Hornblower, looking round him, saw that he was expected to reply in form.

'The Navy,' he said. 'The guardian of the liberties of the world. The unswerving friend, the unremitting enemy. When the tyrant of Europe looks about him, seeking by fair means or foul to extend his dominion, it is the Navy that he finds in his path. It is the Navy which is slowly strangling that tyrant. It is the Navy which has baulked him at every turn, which is draining the life-blood from his boasted Empire and which will bring him down in ruin at the end. The tyrant may boast of unbroken victory on land, but he can only deplore unbroken defeat at sea. It is because of the Navy that every victory only leaves him weaker than before, forced,

like Sisyphus, to roll his rock once more up towards an un-
attainable summit. And one day that rock will crush him.
May it be sooner rather than later!'

Hornblower ended his speech amid a little fierce murmur
from the others at the table. He had hoped when he had first
heard of the intended visit of the Czar to have an opportunity
some time during the day of calling his attention once more
to the aid which the British alliance could afford him. Hornblower stole a glance at the Czar to see if he had attained
his end; Alexander was sitting rapt in thought, his eyes
looking down at the table. He raised them to meet Hornblower's with a smile, and Hornblower felt a wave of exultation, of sublime confidence that his plan had succeeded. He
had had plain fare served at luncheon of set purpose; he had
shown Alexander exactly how the Navy lived and slept and
worked. Alexander would be moved both to help men who
won glory at such a cost and also would desire to have such
tough fighters on his side.

Alexander was making a move to leave; the aide-de-camp
hurriedly drained his fifth tumbler of rum, and it and its pre-
decessors so worked upon him as to make him put his arm
round Bush's shoulders as they came up on the quarter-deck
and pat him on the back with wholehearted affection. Bush,
keenly aware of the eyes of the ship's company upon him,
tried to writhe away from the embrace, but unavailingly. He
was red in the face as he bawled the order for the manning
of the yards, and sighed with evident relief as Alexander's
departure down the accommodation ladder made it necessary
for the aide-de-camp to follow him.

Russia enters the War

The British squadron sailed from Kronstadt next morning to patrol the Baltic. Within a few days news came that Russia had declared war on Bonaparte, and Hornblower had the satisfaction of knowing that his efforts to persuade the Czar to take this bold course had been triumphantly successful. He ordered the cutter Clam home with his despatches describing these vital events, and was grateful for the chance to send back Mr Braun in her, with a report on his attempted assassination of the Czar and Bernadotte that could only lead to his court martial on arrival in England.

The armies of the French and their unwilling allies were already pressing the Russians back from their frontiers, and a section was marching up the Baltic coast to take St Petersburg. The advance of this army, under Marshal Macdonald, the descendant of a Scottish family which had fled to France after Bonnie Prince Charlie's rising, had been halted by Russian resistance along the line of the River Dwina which flowed into the Baltic at Riga, and Hornblower had anchored his squadron in the mouth of the river and offered all the help in his power to the Russians. His arrival in Riga was welcomed with ceremonial honours, for the presence of the British squadron greatly encouraged the defending forces, and on the first evening he accompanied the Governor of the city, General Essen, to a gala performance at the ballet, a form of entertainment in which Hornblower took no pleasure at all. Half-way through the performance the sound of gunfire caused a distraction.

THE firing was very heavy. Somewhere not very far away big guns were being fired rapidly and in large numbers. Hornblower's first thought was for his ships, but he knew them to be safe, anchored at the mouth of the Dwina, and if the wind was still in the direction it was blowing when he entered the theatre Bush could get them out of harm's way whatever happened, even if Riga were taken by storm that very hour.

The audience was taking its cue from the Governor, and as he refused to allow the gunfire to distract him everyone made a brave attempt to appear unconcerned. But everyone in the box, at least, felt tightened nerves when rapid steps outside in the stone-flagged corridor, to the accompaniment of the ringing of spurs, heralded the entrance of an orderly officer, who came in and whispered hurriedly to the Governor. Essen dismissed him with a few words, and only when he had gone, and after a minute's interval which seemed like an hour, leaned over to Hornblower with the news.

'The French have tried to take Daugavgriva by a *coup de main,*' he explained. 'There is no chance of their succeeding.'

That was the village on the left bank of the Dwina, in the angle between the sea and the river, the natural first objective for a besieging force that was desirous of cutting off the town from all hope of relief by sea. It was nearly an island, with the Gulf of Riga covering one flank, and the mile-wide Dwina river covering the rear, while the rest was girt by marshes and ditches and protected by breastworks thrown up by the peasant labour called in from miles round. The French would be likely to try a direct assault upon the place, because success would save them weeks of tedious siege operations, and they had no knowledge as yet of whether or not the Russians were able or willing to offer effective resistance. This was the first time Macdonald had encountered any serious opposition since he had begun his advance across Lithuania—the main Russian armies were contesting the road to Moscow in the neighbourhood of Smolensk. Hornblower had inspected the works that very morning, had observed the strength of the place and the steady appearance of the Russian grenadiers who garrisoned it, and had formed the conclusion that it was safe against anything except systematic siege. Yet he wished he could be as sublimely confident about it as the Governor was.

On the other hand, everything possible had already been done. If the village fell, it fell, and nothing more serious had happened than the loss of an outwork. If the attack were beaten off there could be no question of following up the success, not while Macdonald disposed of sixty thousand men and the Russians of fifteen thousand at most. Of course Macdonald was bound to attempt a *coup de main* upon Daugavgriva. It was interesting to speculate what would be his next move should the assault fail. He might march up the river and endeavour to force a passage above the town, although that meant plunging into a roadless tangle of marsh and attempting a crossing at a place where he would find no boats. Or he might try the other plan and use the boats which had fallen into his hands at Mitau to pass a force across the mouth of the river, leaving Daugavgriva untaken while he compelled the Russians in Riga to choose between coming out and fighting the landing party, or retreating towards St Petersburg, or being shut in completely in the town. It was hard to guess what he would decide on.

Hornblower came back to himself, delighted to find that he had missed in his abstraction some substantial amount of the ballet. He did not know how long his absent-mindedness had endured, but it must be, he thought, for some considerable time. The gunfire had ceased; either the assault had failed or had been completely successful.

At that very moment the door opened to admit another orderly officer with a whispered message for the Governor.

'The attack has been beaten off,' said Essen to Hornblower. 'Yakoulev reports his men have hardly suffered at all, and the front of the place is covered with French and German dead.'

That was to be expected, granted the failure of the attack. The losses would be dreadful in an unsuccessful assault. Macdonald had gambled, risking a couple of thousand lives against a speedy end to the siege, and he had lost.

'We may as well go and see,' said Essen. 'It would not have been well to get up and go when the firing began. But the people will not know now that we left in haste.'

Outside the theatre a troop of hussars sat their horses, while two grooms stood at the heads of two more horses. Essen climbed on to his horse, and Hornblower followed his example. The bright full moon filled the square with light, as, with the escort following, they trotted clattering over the cobbles. Two turns and a moderate descent brought them to the big floating bridge that spanned the Dwina; the road-way over the pontoons drummed hollow beneath the horses' hoofs. Across the river a road ran on the top of a high levée beside the water; on the far side the land was cut and seamed with ditches and ponds, around which twinkled innumerable camp-fires, and here Essen halted and gave an order which sent the hussar officer and half the escort riding ahead of them.

'I have no desire to be shot by my own men,' explained Essen. 'Sentries will be nervous, and riding into a village that has just suffered a night attack will be as dangerous as storming a battery.'

They were challenged repeatedly as they rode along, but despite Essen's gloomy prognostication no jumpy sentry fired at them. Finally they drew up in reply to another challenge at a point where the dome of the church of Daugavgriva stood up black against the pale sky. With the cessation of the noise of the horses' hoofs a fresh sound claimed Hornblower's attention; a wailing clamour coloured by high agonized screams; a whole chorus of groans and cries. The sentry passed them through, and they rode forward into the village, and as they did so the groans and screams were explained, for they passed on their left the torch-lit field where the wounded were being treated—Hornblower had a glimpse of a naked writhing body being held down on a table while the surgeons bent over it in the glare of the torches like the familiars of the Inquisition, while the whole field was carpeted with writhing and groaning wounded.

They dismounted at the door of the church and Essen led the way in, returning the salute of the bearded grenadiers at the door. Candles within made a bright pool of light in the midst of the surrounding gloom, and at a table there sat a group of officers drinking tea from a samovar which hissed beside them. They rose as the Governor entered, and Essen made the introductions.

'General Diebitch. Colonel von Clausewitz—Commodore Sir Hornblower.'

Diebitch was a Pole, Clausewitz a German—the Prussian renegade Hornblower had heard about previously, an intellectual soldier who had decided that true patriotism lay in fighting Bonaparte regardless of which side his country nominally assisted. They made their report in French; the enemy had attempted at moonrise to storm the village without preparation, and had been bloodily repulsed.

'It is only half an hour before dawn, sir,' concluded

Diebitch. 'Would you care to climb to the dome and see for yourself?'

The sky was brighter still by the time they had climbed the narrow stone stair in the thickness of the wall of the church and emerged into the open gallery that encircled it. The whole of the flat marshy countryside was revealed for their inspection, the ditches and the lakes, and the little Mitau river winding its way down from the far distance, through the village almost under the side of the church, to lose itself at the very angle where the vast Dwina entered the bay. The line of breastworks and abattis thrown up by the garrison to defend the left bank of the Dwina was plainly traced, and beyond them could be seen the scanty works which were all that the invaders had bothered to construct up to the moment. The smoke of a thousand cooking-fires drifted over the country.

'In my opinion, sir,' said Clausewitz deferentially, 'if the enemy should decide to proceed by regular siege that is where he will begin. He will trace his first parallel *there,* between the river and that pinewood and sap forward against the village, establishing his batteries on that neck of land *there.* After three weeks' work he could expect to bring his batteries forward on to the glacis and deliver a regular assault. He must effect the reduction of this village before proceeding to the attack on the town.'

'Perhaps,' said Essen.

Hornblower could not imagine a Napoleonic army of sixty thousand men in full march for St Petersburg condescending to spend three weeks in siege operations against an outwork without trying first every extemporary method, like the brusque assault of last night. He borrowed a telescope from one of the staff, and devoted his time to examining the maze of waterways and marshes that stretched before him, and then, walking round the dome along the gallery, he turned his attention to the view of Riga, with its spires, beyond the huge river. Far off, well down the channel, he could just see the masts of his own squadron, where it swung at anchor at the point where the river blended with the Gulf.

A Disappointing Success

HORNBLOWER was asleep in his cabin in the *Nonsuch* when the alarm was given. He awakened to the sharp cry of the watch on deck, and heard the footsteps overhead of the midshipman of the watch running to him with the news. He was fully awake by the time the midshipman pounded on the door and burst in.

'Rocket from *Raven*, sir.'

'Very good,' said Hornblower, swinging his legs out of his cot.

Brown, the good servant, was already in the cabin—God only knew how he had picked up the warning—with a lighted lantern to hang on the deck beam above, and he had trousers and coat ready for Hornblower to pull over his nightshirt. Hornblower rushed up to the dark quarter-deck, cannoning into another hurrying figure as he did so.

'Damn your eyes!' said the figure, in Bush's voice, and then, 'I beg your pardon, sir.'

The ship was alive with the twittering of the pipes as the hands were summoned from their hammocks, and the main-deck resounded with the drumming of bare feet. Montgomery, officer of the watch, was at the starboard rail.

'*Raven* sent up a rocket, sir, two minutes back. Bearin' sou'-by-east.'

'Wind's west-by-north,' decided Bush, looking down into the tiny light of the binnacle.

A westerly wind and a dark blustery night; ideal conditions for Macdonald to try and push a force across the river mouth. He had twenty big river barges, into which he could cram five thousand men and a few guns; if he once managed to push a force of that size across the river the Russian position would be hopelessly turned. On the other hand, if he were to lose a force of that size—five thousand men killed or drowned or prisoners—it would be a staggering blow which might well give him pause and so gain time for the Russians. Hornblower hoped most passionately that the French flotilla had been allowed to thrust its head well into the noose before Cole in the *Raven* gave the alarm.

A shout from the masthead claimed his attention.

'Gunfire to windward, sir!'

From the deck they could just see a pinpoint of flame stab the darkness, and then another one. At anchor on the very edge of the shoals in that direction was the *Raven;* it was her light draught that had dictated her position there. Vickery in *Lotus* guarded the other bank of the river, while *Nonsuch* perforce still lay anchored in the fairway. All the armed boats of the squadron were rowing guard in the mouth of the river—a navy cutter with a three-pounder could be counted on to deal with a river barge, even if the latter did carry three hundred soldiers. But from the direction of the gunfire it looked as if Cole had given the alarm prematurely. Another gun flashed to leeward; the wind prevented them from hearing the sound of it.

'Call my barge,' ordered Hornblower. He felt he could not stay here in useless suspense.

The boat pushed off from the *Nonsuch,* the men tugging at the oars to move the boat in the teeth of the wind. Brown, in the darkness beside Hornblower, felt his captain's restlessness and anxiety.

A tedious quarter of an hour followed, while the boat lurched and pitched over the steep little waves, and the hands slaved away at the oars. The wash of the seas overside and the groaning of the oars against the thole-pins made a monotonous accompaniment to Hornblower's racing thoughts.

'There's a whole lot o' guns firin' now, sir,' reported Brown.

'I can see them,' replied Hornblower.

The darkness was pierced by shot after shot; it was evident that the guard-boats were all clustered round a single victim.

'There's *Raven*, sir. Shall I make for her?'

'No. Steer for the firing.'

The dark shape of the sloop was just visible ahead; Brown put his helm over a little to lay the barge on a course that would take her past the sloop at a cable's length's distance, heading for the gunfire. They had drawn up abeam of the sloop when there came a flash and a roar from her side, and a shot howled close overhead.

'Jesus!' said Brown. 'Ain't the fools got eyes in their heads?'

Presumably the sloop had hailed the passing boat, and, receiving no reply—the hail being carried away by the wind —had incontinently fired. Another shot came from the *Raven,* and someone in the barge squawked with dismay. It was demoralizing to be fired upon by one's own side.

'Turn towards her,' ordered Hornblower. 'Burn a blue light.'

At any moment the sloop might fire a full broadside, with every chance of blowing the barge out of the water. Hornblower took the tiller while Brown wrestled, cursing under his breath, with flint and steel and tinder. The hand pulling at the stroke oar said something to try to quicken his movements.

'Shut your mouth!' snapped Hornblower.

Everything was in a muddle, and the men knew it. Brown caught a spark on the tinder, jabbed the fuse of the blue light upon it, and then blew the fuse into a glow. A moment later the firework burst into an unearthly glare, lighting up the boat and the water round it, and Hornblower stood up so that his features and his uniform should be visible to the sloop. It was poor revenge to think of the consternation in the *Raven* when they saw that they had been firing on their own Commodore. Hornblower went up the sloop's side in a state of cold fury. Cole was there to receive him, of course.

'Well, Mr Cole?'

'Sorry I fired on you, sir, but you didn't answer my hail.'

'Did it occur to you that with this wind blowing I could not hear you?'

'Yes, sir. But we know the French are out. The boats fired on them an hour back, and half my crew is away in the boats. Supposing I were boarded by two hundred French soldiers? I couldn't take chances, sir.'

It was no use arguing with a man as jumpy and as nervous as Cole evidently was.

'You sent up the alarm rocket?'

'Yes, sir. I had to inform you that the barges were at sea.'

'You did that the first moment you knew?'

'Yes, sir. Of course, sir.'

'Did it occur to you that you would alarm the French as well?'

'I thought that was what you wanted, sir.'

Hornblower turned away in disgust. The man in his excitement had clean forgotten every order given him.

'Boat approaching from to wind'ard, sir,' reported someone, his white shirt just visible in the gathering dawn. Cole ran forward excitedly, with Hornblower striding after him,

There came a flash and a roar from her side

catching up to him as he stood at the knightheads staring at the boat.

'Boat ahoy!' yelled Cole through his speaking trumpet.

'Aye aye,' came the answering hail downwind. That was the correct reply for an approaching boat with officers on board. She was a ship's cutter under a dipping lugsail; as Hornblower watched she took in the sail with considerable clumsiness and came dropping down to the sloop under oars. Level with the bow she turned, clumsily again, and headed in to lie alongside the sloop. Hornblower could see she was crammed with men.

'Soldiers!' suddenly exclaimed Cole, pointing at the boat with an excited forefinger. 'Stand to your guns, men! Sheer off, there!'

Hornblower could see shakoes and crossbelts; it must be just the kind of vision Cole's imagination had been toying with all through the night. A reassuring English voice came back to them from overside.

'Avast, there! This is *Lotus's* cutter with prisoners.'

It was Purvis's voice without a doubt. Hornblower walked to the waist and looked down. There was Purvis in the stern, and British seamen in check shirts at the oars, but every inch of space was filled with soldiers, sitting in attitudes of apprehension or dejection.

'Let 'em come up,' said Hornblower.

They climbed the side, greeted by the grinning seamen as they reached the deck, and stared round in the growing light. Purvis swung himself up and touched his hat to Hornblower.

'They're all Dutchmen, I think, sir. Not Frogs. We got 'em off the barge we caught. Had to fire into 'em a long time —just shot the barge to pieces, us an' the other boats. They're following us, sir, with the other prisoners.'

'You only caught one barge?'

'Yes, sir. The others ran for home the moment the rocket went up. But we got two hundred prisoners, I should think, an' we had to kill nigh on a hundred more.'

One single barge taken, with two hundred men, when Hornblower had hoped for a dozen barges at least and three thousand men! But Purvis in his innocence was obviously delighted with his capture.

'Here's one of their officers, sir.'

Hornblower turned on the blue-coated man who was wearily climbing over the side.

'Who are you, sir?' he asked in French, and after a moment's hesitation the officer replied haltingly in the same language.

'Lieutenant von Bulow, of the Fifty-first Regiment of Infantry.'

'French infantry?'

'Of the King of Prussia,' said the officer, sternly, with a Teutonic explosiveness in the word 'Prusse' which indicated his annoyance at the suggestion that he would be a Frenchman.

So Macdonald had not risked French lives in his highly dangerous venture; that was to be expected, of course. Bonaparte had made war largely at the expense of his allies for the last ten years.

'I will see that you are given refreshment,' said Hornblower, politely. 'Please order your men to sit down against the rail there.'

Most of them were wet and bedraggled, apparently having been in the water before surrendering. Hornblower gave orders for them to be fed, at the same time as the other boats came back downwind, each with its quota of prisoners. On the cramped decks of the *Raven* the two hundred prisoners made a fine show; Cole had the two foremost chase-guns run

inboard and trained round upon them, a round of canister
in each gun, the gun-captains posted with lighted matches
ready to fire into them. Seamen, still grinning, went along
their ranks handing out bread and beer.

'See how they eat, sir!' said Purvis. 'Look at that one,
layin' into his biscuit like a wolf with a bone. God damme,
it's gone a'ready. It's true what they say, sir, about Boney
never feedin' his men.'

An Imperial army was wont to gather its food from the
countryside as it marched; Macdonald's sixty thousand had
been stationary now for over two weeks, and in a thinly-
populated country. They must be on short commons. Every
day the siege of Riga could be prolonged would cost lives in
plenty to Bonaparte, and although he was ever prodigal with
lives there must come a time at last when he would have no
more to spare, not even Prussian ones, or Italian ones. The
greater the pity, then, that the whole division that had tried
to pass the river had not been wiped out.

The Bomb-Ketches gain Four Days

HORNBLOWER was once more up in the gallery that encircled the dome of the church of Daugavgriva.

'You see what I was telling you about, sir,' said Clausewitz, pointing.

Out beyond the Russian works stretched a long line, brown against the green, the parapet of the trench the French had thrown up during the night. Macdonald must be a general with energy, for he had had this work done at the same time as he had sent the Prussians on their risky endeavour to cross the river, so that while one attempt had failed he had made a solid gain, profiting by the dark and rainy night to throw up this entrenchment far forward unobserved.

'That is his first parallel, sir, and in the centre of it is the battery he is constructing. And see there, sir? That is where he is sapping forward.'

Hornblower stared through his telescope. At a point towards the end of the face of the first parallel he could see something that looked like a wall constructed of bundles of timber. The guns in the Russian works far below him were firing at it; he could see earth flying as the shots struck round it. At the end of the wall of timber was something that looked strange—a sort of shield on wheels. He was studying it when he saw it moved out suddenly, leaving a narrow gap between it and the end of the timber wall, in which for a fleeting moment he saw a couple of men in blue uniforms. It was only a fleeting moment, for immediately the gap was filled with a new bundle of timber. Above the new bundle he could see the blades of spades rising and then disappearing; apparently the bundle of timber was hollow, barrel-shaped, and as soon as it was in position the men sheltering behind it set to work to fill it up with earth dug from behind it. Hornblower realized that he was witnessing the classic method of sapping towards an enemy's position with 'gabion' and 'fascine.' That big timber basket was a gabion, now being filled with earth. Farther back, under cover of the line of filled gabions, the besiegers were revetting their breastwork with fascines, six-foot bundles of wood, and farther back still they were building the whole thing solid with earth dug from a trench behind the breastwork. As he watched, the shield was suddenly pushed forward another yard, and another gabion was put in position; the French were three feet nearer the earthworks which guarded Daugavgriva. No, not a yard, a little less, because the sap was not pointing straight at its objective, but out at its flank so that it could not be enfiladed. Soon it would change its direction, and point towards the other flank, approaching the fortress in zigzag fashion, ruthlessly and remorselessly. Of all operations of war a scientific siege was the most certain if relief did not arrive from the outside.

'See there, sir!' said Clausewitz suddenly.

From behind a high embankment had suddenly emerged a long string of horses, looking like ants at that distance, but the white breeches of the men who led them showed up clearly in the sunshine. The horses were dragging a cannon, a big piece of artillery when its apparent size was compared with that of the horses. It crawled towards the battery in the centre of the first parallel, a myriad white-breeched specks attending it. The high breastwork of the first parallel screened the operation from the sight of the Russian gunners and shielded it from their fire.

'They will have that battery armed by to-morrow,' said Clausewitz. 'And look! There is another gabion put in place.'

Siege operations had the remorseless cold inevitability of the advance of a snake on a paralysed bird.

'Why do your guns not stop the work on the sap?' asked Hornblower.

'They are trying, as you see. But a single gabion is not an easy target to hit at this range, and it is only the end one which is vulnerable. And by the time the sap approaches within easy range their battery-fire will be silencing our guns.'

Another siege-gun had made its appearance from behind the high embankment, and was crawling towards the battery; its predecessor was at that moment being thrust finally into its position at the breastwork.

'Can you not bring your ships up, sir?' asked Clausewitz. 'See how the water comes close to their works there. You could shoot them to pieces with your big guns.'

Hornblower shook his head; the same idea had already occurred to him, for the long glittering arm of the Gulf of Riga which reached into the land there was very tempting. But there was less than a fathom of water in it, and even his shallow bomb-ketches drew nine feet—seven at least if he emptied them of all their stores save those necessary for the action.

'I would do so if I could,' said Hornblower, 'but at the present moment I can see no means of getting my guns into range.'

Clausewitz looked at him coldly, and Hornblower was conscious that goodwill between allies was a frail thing. Earlier that morning British and Russians had been the best of friends; Essen and Clausewitz had been thoroughly elated at the turning back of Macdonald's attempt to cross the river, and had thought that the annihilation of a half-battalion of Prussians a notable success, not knowing of the far more far-reaching plan which Hornblower had made and which Cole's nervousness had brought to almost naught. When affairs went well, allies were the best of friends, but in adversity each naturally tended to blame the other. Now that the French approaches were moving towards Daugravgriva he was asking why the Russian artillery did not stop them, and the Russians were asking why his ships' guns did not do the same.

Hornblower made his explanation as fully as he could, but Clausewitz turned an unsympathetic ear, and so did Essen when the matter came up for discussion as Hornblower was saying good-bye to him. It was a poor showing for a Navy whose boast was that nothing was impossible; Hornblower was irritable and snappy when he returned that afternoon to the *Nonsuch*.

He went out into the quarter gallery, and, bowed below the overhanging cove above, he tried to stride up and down its twelve-foot length. It was indeed a pity that he could not bring his ships' guns to bear on the siege-works. Heavy guns at close range would play havoc with the French breastworks. And behind the high dyke from which he had seen the guns being dragged must lie the French park and train—a few shells from the bomb-vessels would wreak havoc there, and if only he could get the ketches up the bay it would be easy to drop shells over the dyke. But over most of the bay there was only three or four feet of water, and nowhere more than seven. The thing was impossible, and the best thing he could do was to forget about it. To distract himself he stepped over the rail into the other quarter gallery, and peeped through the stern window into Bush's cabin. Bush was asleep on his cot, flat on his back with his mouth open, his hands spread wide at his sides and his wooden leg hanging in a becket against the bulkhead. Hornblower felt a twinge of annoyance that his captain should be sleeping so peacefully while he himself had so many cares on his shoulders.

He stepped back into his own quarter gallery, and as he did, as he stood with one leg suspended and with the rudder gudgeons creaking a little in their pintles in the stream below him, the idea came to him, so that he stood stock still for a space, with one leg in mid-air. Then he brought his leg over and walked into his cabin and shouted for a messenger.

'My compliments to the officer of the watch, and will he please signal to *Harvey* for Mr Mound to come on board at once.'

Mound came down into the cabin, young and expectant, and yet with his eagerness thinly overlaid with assumed nonchalance.

'Mr Mound, do you know of the progress of the French siege-works?'

'No, sir.'

'Then look at this chart with me. They have a line of trenches here, with a battery here. Their main flank and stores are behind a dyke, here. If we could bring the bomb-vessels up the bay we could shell them out of both places.'

'Shoal water, sir,' said Mound regretfully.

'Yes,' said Hornblower, and for the life of him he could not stop himself from making a dramatic pause before uttering the crucial word. 'But with camels we could reduce the draught.'

'Camels!' exclaimed Mound, and as he realized all the implications his face lit up. 'By George, sir, you're right.'

Camels are a means of reducing the draught of a ship— loaded vessels lashed tightly one on each side and then emptied, so as to raise the centre ship further out of the water. Mound was already grappling with the details.

'There are lighters and barges in Riga, sir. They'll give us some, sure as a gun. Plenty of sand to ballast 'em, or we can fill 'em with water and pump 'em out. With two big lighters I could lessen *Harvey's* draught by five feet easy—lift her clear out of the water for that matter. Those lighters are two hundred tons burden an' don't draw more than a couple of feet empty.'

A difficulty had occurred to Hornblower while Mound was speaking, one which he had not thought of before.

'How are you going to steer 'em all?' he demanded. 'They'll be unmanageable.'

'Rig a Danube rudder, sir,' replied Mound instantly. 'Make it big enough and you could steer anything with one.'

'I'll send a note to the Governor,' said Hornblower, 'asking for the loan of four lighters. I'll make it six, in case of accidents. Have your plans ready in an hour's time. You can draw upon this ship and the sloops for the materials and men you'll need.'

'Aye aye, sir.'

There was need for haste, for that very evening there came sullenly booming across the bay the sound of heavy guns firing, and the next morning, just as Hornblower came out on the quarter-deck, there was a sudden loud crash ashore, like a peal of thunder, to herald the opening salvo of the enemy. Its echoes had not died away before a more ragged salvo succeeded it, and then another more ragged still, and so on until the air was ceaselessly tormented by the loud reports, like a continuous thunderstorm from which the ear waited continually for relief that was not granted it. The masthead lookout reported a long smear of smoke drifted by the breeze across the countryside from the enemy's battery.

'Call away my barge,' said Hornblower.

At *Nonsuch's* boat booms there already lay an assortment of the boats of the squadron, piled high with the stores which had been taken out of the two bomb-ketches. The barge danced over the water in the sparkling dawn to where the bomb-ketches lay anchored, each with a lighter on either side. Duncan, captain of the *Moth,* was being rowed round the group in a jolly boat. He touched his hat as the barge approached.

'Morning, sir,' he said, and then instantly turned back to the work in hand, raising his speaking-trumpet to his lips. 'Too much by the bows! Take up the for'ard cable another pawl!'

Hornblower had himself rowed on to the *Harvey,* and leaped from his barge to the lighter on her starboard side—not much of a leap, because she was laden down with ballast—without bothering officers or men for compliments. Mound was standing on his tiny quarter-deck, testing with his foot the tension of the big cable—one of *Nonsuch's*—which was frapped round his own ship and both lighters, two turns round each, forward and aft.

'Carry on, port side!' he yelled.

In each of the lighters a large working party was stationed, the men equipped with shovels for the most part extemporized out of wood. At Mound's order the men in the port-side lighter recommenced lustily shovelling the sand over the side. Clouds of it drifted astern on the faint wind. Mound tested the tension again.

'Carry on, starboard side!' he yelled again, and then, perceiving his Commodore approaching, he came to the salute.

'Good morning, Mr Mound,' said Hornblower.

'Good morning, sir. We have to do this part of it step by step, you see, sir. I have the old ketch so light she'll roll over in the cables if I give her the chance.'

'I understand, Mr Mound.'

'The Russians were prompt enough sending out the lighters to us, sir.'

'Can you wonder?' replied Hornblower. 'D'you hear the French battery at work?'

Mound listened and apparently heard it for the first time. He had been engrossed too deeply in his work to pay any attention to it before; his face was unshaven and grey with fatigue, for his activity had not ceased since Hornblower had summoned him the afternoon before. In that time both ketches had been emptied of their stores, the cables roused out and got across to them, the lighters received and laid alongside in the dark, and each group of three vessels bound into a single mass with the cables hauled taut by the capstans.

'Excuse me, sir,' said Mound, and ran forward to examine the forward cable.

Hornblower went back to his barge and rowed over to the *Moth*. The work here was a stage more advanced; so much sand had been shovelled out of the lighters that it was only with slow effort that the working parties could heave their shovelfuls over the side, shoulder-high. A wide streak of the *Moth's* copper was already visible, so high was she riding.

'Watch your trim, Mr Duncan,' said Hornblower. 'She's canting a little to port.'

'Aye aye, sir.'

It called for some complicated adjustment of the cables, veering out and hauling in, to set *Moth* on an even keel again.

'Two hours more an' they'll be clear, sir,' reported Duncan. 'Then we'll only have to pierce the sides for sweeps.'

He glanced over at the sun, still not far above the horizon.

'We'll be ready for action half an hour before noon, sir,' he added.

While the sides of the lighters were being pierced Hornblower called Duncan and Mound to him and went over their final orders with them.

'I'll be up in the church with the signalling party,' he said in conclusion. 'I'll see that you're properly supported. So good luck.'

'Thank you, sir,' they answered in unison. Excitement and anticipation masked their weariness.

So Hornblower had himself rowed over to the village, where a tiny jetty saved him and the signallers from splashing through the shallows; the roar of the bombardment and the counter-bombardment grew steadily louder as they approached.

The village was already badly knocked about, great holes showing in the walls and roofs of the flimsy cottages of which it was composed. As they neared the church Hornblower swung round to a sudden unusual noise to see his two mid-

shipmen standing staring at the headless corpse of a seaman
who a moment before had been walking at their heels. A ball
flying over the earthworks had shattered his head to atoms
and flung his body against them. Somers was eyeing with
disgust the blood and brains which had spattered his white
trousers.

'Come along,' said Hornblower.

In the gallery under the dome they could look down upon
the siege. The zigzag approach trench was almost half-way
towards the defences, the head of it almost obscured by flying
earth as the Russians fired furiously upon it. But the central
redoubt which covered the entrance to the village was in bad
shape, its parapets battered into nothing more than mounds,
a gun lying half buried beside its shattered carriage, although
the other one was still being worked by a devoted little group.
The whole of the French works were obscured by the thin
pall of smoke which spread from the breaching battery, but
the smoke was not so thick as to hide a column of infantry
marching down towards the first parallel from the rear.

'They relieve the guard of the trenches at noon,' explained
Clausewitz. 'Where are these boats of yours, sir?'

'Here they come,' said Hornblower.

They were creeping over the silvery water, fantastic in
appearance, the ketches with their sails furled and the ugly
bulks of the lighters beside them. The long clumsy sweeps,
a dozen on each side, looked like the legs of a water-boatman
on a pond, but far slower in movement as the toiling seamen
who manned them tugged them through each successive
endless stroke.

'Somers! Gerard!' said Hornblower, sharply. 'How are
your signalling arrangements working out? Lash those blocks
to the cornice up there. Come along, you haven't all day to
get ready in.'

The midshipmen and seamen addressed themselves to the business of making a signalling station up on the gallery. The blocks were lashed to the cornice and the halliards rove through them, the Russian staff watching the operation with interest. Meanwhile the bomb-ketches came crawling up the bay, painfully slow under their sweeps; no one among the enemy seemed to be paying them the least attention; Bonaparte's armies, lords of Europe from Madrid to Smolensk, had had few opportunities of becoming acquainted with bomb-ketches. The firing from the big battery went on steadily, pounding at the crumbling Russian earthworks below, with the Russians returning the fire with desperate energy.

The *Harvey* and the *Moth* came creeping in until they were quite close to shore; Hornblower through his glass could see minute figures moving in their bows, and knew they were dropping their anchors. The sweeps worked spasmodically, first on one side and then on the other—they were placing themselves in position to drop other anchors at the stern, so that by veering and hauling in on their cables they could swing themselves so as to be able to point their mortars anywhere along a wide arc. Hornblower saw the stern anchors let go, and could see little groups of men bending to work at the capstans; the bomb-ketches turned almost imperceptibly first this way and then that as their captains trained them round by the aid of the leading marks on the shore.

'There's the "ready" flag going up in *Harvey*,' said Hornblower, the glass at his eye.

The sheave in the block above his head shrilled noisily as the halliard ran over it, bearing the acknowledgment. A big puff of smoke suddenly spurted upwards from the *Harvey's* bows; Hornblower at that distance could see nothing of the shell in its flight, and he waited nervously, compelling himself to search the whole area round about the battery to make sure of seeing the burst. And he saw nothing, nothing at all. Reluctantly he ordered hoisted the black cone for 'unobserved' and *Harvey* fired again. This time he could see the burst, a little volcano of smoke and fragments just beyond the battery.

'That was over, sir,' said Somers.

'Yes. Make that to *Harvey*.'

Duncan had anchored *Moth* by now, and was flying the signal of readiness. *Harvey's* next shell fell square in the centre of the battery, and immediately afterwards *Moth's* first shell did the same. At once the two ketches began a systematic bombardment of the battery, dropping shells into it in constant succession, so that there was not a moment when a fountain of smoke and earth was not apparent within its earthworks. It was a plain rectangular structure, without traverses or internal subdivisions, and there was no shelter for the men within it now that their enemy had found means to circumvent their earthworks. They only maintained their fire for a few seconds, and then Hornblower could see them running from their guns; the interior of the battery looked like a disturbed ants' nest. One of the big thirteen-inch shells landed full on the parapet, and the smoke clearing away revealed the breastwork blown flat, opening the interior of the battery to view from ground level in the village, and through the gap was visible the muzzle of a dismounted siege-gun, pointed skyward and helpless—a cheering sight for the defence. That was only the beginning. Gap after gap was blown in the earthworks; the whole interior was plastered with shells. At one moment there was a much bigger explosion than usual, and Hornblower guessed that an 'expense magazine'—the small store of gunpowder kept in the battery and continually replenished from the rear—had blown up. Down below him the defence had taken new heart, and every gun along the menaced front had reopened fire; it was a shot from the village, apparently, which hit the muzzle of the dismounted gun and flung it back upon the ground.

'Signal "cease fire," ' said Hornblower.

Thirteen-inch shells were not munitions of war that could be readily obtained in the Baltic, and there was no purpose in wasting them upon a target which was silenced and at least made temporarily useless. And then came the countermove on the part of the attack, as he had expected. A battery of field artillery was coming over the distant slope, six guns, minute at that distance, jolting and swaying after their limbers.

'Signal for the target to change,' ordered Hornblower.

There was no means of observing the fall of the shells on the new target, for the bomb-ketches were dropping them just over the high dyke. It was a matter of chance should they do any destruction, but Hornblower could guess that the park and depots of an army of sixty thousand men conducting a first-class siege were likely to be both extensive and crowded; a few shells dropped there might do good. The first field battery was approaching the water's edge, the horses wheeling round to leave the guns pointing at the bomb-ketches at neat geometrical intervals.

'*Harvey* signals she's shifting target, sir,' reported Gerard.

'Very good.'

Harvey was firing at the field battery; it took her a little while to get the range, and field-guns, spaced far part in a long thin line, were not a good target for mortars, even though the fall of the shells was now under direct observation. And a second battery was coming up on the flank of the first and— Hornblower's telescope could easily make them out across the narrow extremity of the bay—there were more guns coming into action to put the bomb-vessels under a cross-fire. One of *Harvey's* shells burst close beside one of the guns, presumably killing every man serving it, but by chance leaving the gun itself still on its wheels. The other guns had opened fire, the smoke creeping lazily from their muzzles. Across the bay the other field batteries were coming into action, although at very long range for field artillery. There was no purpose in continuing to expose the bomb-ketches to the fire of the shore; Macdonald had two hundred field-guns, and there were only two bomb-ketches.

'Signal "Discontinue the action," ' ordered Hornblower.

Now that he had given the word it seemed to him that he had waited over-long. It seemed ages before the bomb-ketches got their anchors hoisted, and Hornblower could see, as he waited anxiously, the splashes thrown up all round them by the shots from the shore. He saw the sweeps thrust out from the sides of the lighters take a grip on the water, swinging the vessels round, and then the white sails mounted the masts, and the queer craft sailed away out of range, making vast leeway which caused them to head crabwise aslant of their course. Hornblower turned away with relief to meet the eyes of the Governor, who had been standing silently watching the whole operation through a vast telescope which he had mounted upon the shoulder of a patient orderly whose back must have ached with crouching.

'Excellent, sir,' said the Governor. 'I thank you, in the name of the Czar. Russia is grateful to you, sir, and so is the city of Riga.'

'Thank you, Your Excellency,' said Hornblower.

Diebitch and Clausewitz were awaiting his attention. They were eager to discuss future operations with him, and he had to listen to them. The conversation was continually interrupted by the coming and going of orderlies with messages, and hasty orders given in languages that he could not understand. But the results of those orders were soon apparent; two regiments of infantry came filing up through the village, with bayonets fixed, lined the earthworks, and then dashed out on the glacis with a yell. The heavy guns in the battery which should have torn them to pieces with grapeshot were all silent; Hornblower watched the sortie reach the approach trench almost without opposition; the men burst into it over the parapets, and hurriedly began to tear down the sandbags and gabions with which it was constructed, while down into the ruined battery came a French infantry force too late to stop them, even if they had been able to do so under the artillery fire of the besieged. In an hour the work was done, the approach trench levelled over large sections, the tools taken, spare gabions heaped together and set on fire.

'Thanks to you, sir,' said Clausewitz, 'the progress of the siege has been delayed by four days.'

A Dawn Landing turns the Enemy's Flank

HORNBLOWER reached for the despatch which had just arrived from the Admiralty, and read once more the passage which had the greatest bearing on the present moment.

Their Lordships desire me to call your particular notice to the fact that Government attaches the greatest importance to maintaining the defence of Riga as long as it is possible. They instruct me that they consider the safety of the squadron under your command as

*secondary compared with the prolongation of the siege
and they charge you, on your peril, to do everything in
your power to prevent the enemy from continuing his
march on St Petersburg.*

In other words, thought Hornblower, Riga must be
defended to the last man—and ship—and they would shoot
him if they thought he had not done his utmost. He shouted
for his barge, locked his desk, seized his hat and, after a
moment's hesitation, his pistols, and had himself rowed once
more over to Daugavgriva.

The village was now a mere mass of ruins, save for the
church, whose solid walls had withstood the flames that had
swept the place and the continual storm of ricochetting shots
which came over from the bombardment of the ramparts.
The place stank of death, for the dead were many and the
earth over them scanty. Trenches had been driven from cellar
to cellar of the ruined houses to permit of safe passage
through the village, and it was by way of these that he made
his way to the church. From the gallery there the view was
ominous. The besiegers' second parallel was completed, no
more than two hundred yards from the defences, and the
approaches were continuing their remorseless progress towards the ditch. The fire from the big battery was ceaseless,
and there was but small reply from the ramparts; too many
gunners had been killed and too many guns knocked to pieces.
Down at the water's edge on the besiegers' side a well-con-
structed battery displayed the guns that were ready to sweep
the area where the bomb-ketches had anchored; there was
no chance of repeating the surprise bombardment of the
breaching battery which had prolonged the siege for four
days.

Clausewitz commented coolly on the situation to Hornblower as they looked at all this through their glasses. To a doctrinaire soldier a siege was an intellectual exercise. It was mathematically possible to calculate the rate of progress of the approaches and the destructive effect of the batteries, to predict every move and countermove in advance, and to foretell within an hour the moment of the final assault. The time had come, now that it was impossible to maintain fire upon the head of the sap, to attempt to delay the progress of the besiegers by a sortie.

'But,' expostulated Hornblower, 'if the French know that a sortie is due, will not they make preparations for it?'

'Yes,' said Clausewitz, his cold grey eyes expressionless.

'Would it not be better to surprise them?'

'Yes. But in a siege how is that to be done?'

'We surprised them with the bomb-vessels.'

'Yes. But now——'

Clausewitz indicated the battery which denied the end of the bay to them.

'But still——' began Hornblower, and then bit off the sentence. There was no purpose in being critical without having a helpful suggestion to make at the same time. He turned his attention once more to the siege-works, looking for inspiration, while the guns roared out below him. In the centre of the second parallel was a new battery, the fire from whose guns would cut up any force attacking frontally in the hope of destroying the works. It would be asking much of any sallying force to cross two hundred yards of naked glacis in the teeth of such a fire and then storm ditch and parapet. The flanks were secure, too, one guarded by the little river and the other trending back towards the bay. The bay! The French batteries might be able to sweep the bay sufficiently effectively to prevent bomb-vessels anchoring there in daylight, but they would not be able to stop an infantry attack launched from boats at night. Then the parallel could be rushed at dawn from the flank. Hornblower turned to Clausewitz with the suggestion, and Clausewitz adopted it instantly. These continental soldiers were always liable to forget about the sea when making their plans, but Clausewitz, Prussian though he was, was a man of sufficient elasticity of mind still to be able to see the merits of a plan based on command of the sea.

There was no time to be lost if the assault upon Daugavgriva were to be anticipated. The plan had to be given form instantly; time-tables worked out, signals agreed upon, troops allocated for the landing and marched to the point where Hornblower could have boats' crews ready to man the river barges which were to carry the troops to the point selected for landing. Hornblower had to detail crews and officers, issue his orders, and make sure they were understood. Montgomery and Duncan, Purvis and Carlin, had to be sent for, brought up to the dome and shown the objectives to be aimed at. Mounted messengers, riding in hot haste, brought back a trio of Russian colonels to the gallery; it was their regiments which were detailed to make the landing. Hornblower explained to them in French, and then explained to his officers in English. Then he had the job of interpreting the questions which everyone wanted to ask. Half a dozen Russian subalterns, squatting on the floor of the gallery nursing pieces of board on which sheets of paper were pinned, wrote out the orders which Clausewitz dictated to them.

It was before noon that Hornblower had made the suggestion to Clausewitz; it was eight in the evening, and the sun had set, before everything was completed, before Hornblower had had himself rowed to the Dwina mouth to inspect the boats which had been provided, and to watch the Russian grenadiers marching down to be herded into them.

'You understand your orders, Duncan?' asked Horn-blower.

'Yes, sir.'

'Let's see your watch. Set it by mine.'

'Aye aye, sir.'

'Mr Montgomery. Mr Purvis. Remember what I said about keeping the landing force together. You must strike all at once—no landing in driblets. Make sure the soldiers know the direction in which to advance when they land.'

'Aye aye, sir.'

'Good luck, then.'

'Thank you, sir.'

It was quite dark by the time Hornblower set foot again on the little jetty at Daugavgriva; dark, and there was a chilly breath in the air. So far had the year advanced since he had first cast anchor in Riga Bay. Midsummer had gone and autumn was at hand. He had to feel his way along the trenches and up to the church, and his legs felt hardly strong enough to carry him up the interminable dark stairs to the gallery.

'The French seem unusually active to-night,' was Clause-witz's greeting to him. 'At dusk they changed the guard of their trenches.'

A string of bright orange flames suddenly lit up the French lines, and the roar of a salvo reached their ears.

'They are periodically spraying the ditch with grape,' explained Clausewitz, 'to hinder our repair parties. It is what is always done, but after half a dozen rounds they lose direction and range.'

If siege warfare was such a mechanical art, if every step was obvious and could be foreseen, there was always the chance of an original-minded general breaking the rules. In two days the breaches and approaches would be ripe for an assault—

what was to prevent an assailant from making his attack a little prematurely and catching the defender off his guard? Hornblower made the suggestion to Clausewitz.

'It is always possible,' said Clausewitz, pontifically. 'But our trench guards are unusually strong to-night because of the sortie at dawn.'

Hornblower felt round in the gloom, and found one of the trusses of straw which had been carried up to the gallery in an endeavour to make this advanced headquarters more comfortable. He sat down gratefully, for his legs were actually trembling with fatigue. He wrapped his cloak closer round him against the chill of the night, and the thought of sleep became inexpressibly alluring.

'I shall rest a while,' he announced, and lay back and closed his eyes. He settled himself down in the straw, and even the tumultuous dreams that assailed him were (as he was somehow aware) not nearly so serious as the thoughts from which he would have suffered had he been awake.

He awoke to Clausewitz's arm on his shoulder.

'An hour before dawn,' said Clausewitz, still only a vague shadow in the brooding darkness.

Hornblower sat up; he was stiff, and had grown cold under the inadequate cover of his cloak. The landing force, if all had gone well, must be creeping up the bay now. It was too dark to see anything as he peered over the parapet of the gallery. The faint report of a single musket-shot reached his ears, and Clausewitz began a remark to him which was cut short by a violent outburst of firing down in no-man's-land between the trench systems. The darkness was spangled with points of flame.

'Possibly patrols with a fit of nerves,' said Clausewitz, but the firing showed no signs of dying down. Instead, it grew in violence. There was a great spearhead of flame down below, pointing towards an irregular mass of flashes, where apparently a column was meeting a line. The flashes flared up and died away with the ragged volleys; soon cannons were contributing their orange flames, and immediately afterwards there was more fire as blazing combustibles—carcasses— were flung by attackers and defenders from the parapets to illuminate their enemies. From the bay arose a curving streak of yellow fire, soaring upwards towards the sky, and then bursting into scarlet stars.

'Thank God for that!' said Hornblower, but he kept the words to himself.

The landing party had reached their station a little ahead of their time, and somebody, English or Russian, had sensibly decided to launch the flank attack immediately upon seeing the firing ashore. Clausewitz turned and rapped out an order which sent an aide-de-camp hurrying down the stairs. At almost the same moment a messenger came running up, gabbling Russian so rapidly that Clausewitz, with his limited command of the language, had to make him repeat his words more slowly. When the message was delivered he turned to Hornblower.

'The enemy is in strong force, apparently intending to make a surprise attack. He might save two days if it were successful.'

A fresh tumult broke out down below; the landing party had encountered their first opposition, and the invisible landscape towards the shore was spangled with a new pattern of flashes. There was a desperate battle going on, where attackers and counter-attackers and the flank attack drove together; there was a faint light beginning to show now, but still nothing could be seen of the fighting, save for vague smoke-clouds drifting in the semi-darkness. The clatter of musketry and the crash of artillery told of the bitter struggle, and once Hornblower heard a deep shout from many throats answered by a wild yell. That was when some attack met a counter-attack, presumably. Steadily the landscape grew brighter, and the messengers began to pour in.

'Shevstoff has stormed the battery guarding the shore,' said Clausewitz, exultantly.

Shevstoff was the general commanding the landing party. If he had stormed the battery the boats' crews would be able to effect an unmolested retreat, while the arrival of a messenger from him here in Daugavgriva meant that he was in full touch with the defenders, and presumably his force had executed its orders and fallen on the flank of the French position. The firing seemed to be dying away, even though the smoke still blended with the low ground-mist of autumn and kept everything concealed.

'Kladoff is in the approaches,' went on Clausewitz. 'His workmen are breaking down the parapets.'

The firing increased again, although now there was so much light that no flashes were visible. A frightful death-struggle was apparently going on, so desperate that the arrival of the Governor in the gallery attracted little attention from the group straining to see through the fog and smoke.

Essen gathered the details with a few quick questions to Clausewitz, and then he turned to Hornblower.

'I would have been here an hour ago,' he said, 'but I was detained by the arrival of despatches.'

Essen's massive countenance was gloomy; he took Hornblower's arm and drew him out of earshot of the junior staff officers.

'Bad news?' asked Hornblower.

'Yes. The worst. We have been beaten in a great battle outside Moscow, and Bonaparte is in the city.'

That was the worst of news indeed. Hornblower could

foresee a future time when he supposed that battle would rank along with Marengo and Austerlitz and Jena, as a smashing victory which laid a nation low, and the entry into Moscow would rank with the occupation of Vienna and Berlin. A week or two more and Russia would sue for peace and England would be left alone, with the whole world in arms against her. Hornblower forced himself to take the blow impassively, forced his face to bear no hint of dismay.

'We shall fight it out here all the same,' he said.

'Yes,' said Essen, 'my men will fight to the last. So will my officers.'

There was almost a grin on his face as he jerked his head towards Clausewitz; that was a man who had his neck in a noose if ever a man had, fighting against his own country.

The mist and smoke were thinning, and patches of the field of battle were visible now, and Hornblower and Essen turned their attention to the work in hand as if with relief from contemplating the future.

'Ha!' said Essen, pointing.

Portions of the approaches were in plain view, and here and there were jagged gaps in the parapets.

'Kladoff has carried out his orders, sir,' said Clausewitz.

Until those gaps were repaired, one by one, starting with the gap nearest the first parallel, no one would be able to reach the head of the sap, and certainly no strong force could use the approaches. Another two days had been won, decided Hornblower, gauging the amount of destruction with his eye—experience had brought him facility already in appreciating siege operations. There was still heavy firing going on as the rearguard covered the retreat of the sallying forces to the ramparts.

Down in the shattered remains of the village, as he walked

along the trenches, those of the wounded who had been fortunate enough to drag themselves back were receiving treatment. Shuddering, Hornblower pushed past ranks of smoke-blackened and ragged Russian soldiers, talking with the noisy abandon of men who have just emerged from a hard-won victory.

Hornblower leads a Counter-Charge

AMONG the mass of long-delayed mail from England were great packets of printed pamphlets in French and in German, a few even in Dutch and in Danish. They were appeals to Bonaparte's forces to desert his standard—not suggestions for mass desertions, but intended for the individual soldier, telling him that he could be sure of a welcome if he were to come over. They offered a life of ease and security, with the honourable alternative, only if requested, of enlistment in the British forces, to those who wished to strike a blow against the tyrant.

The usually well-fed and well-cared-for Prussians under Macdonald's command were on meagre rations now that the country round had been stripped bare by foragers; an offer of a life of well-fed ease combined with an appeal to their patriotism might bring in deserters in plenty. Hornblower mapped out in his mind a formal letter to the Governor in which he would suggest that a few pedlars be sent into the French camp ostensibly to sell luxuries but really to distribute these pamphlets.

Someone knocked at the door.

'Come in,' bellowed Hornblower, irritated at the interruption, for he had intended to spend all day catching up on his arrears of paper work.

'A letter from the beach, sir,' said the midshipman of the watch.

It was a brief note from the Governor with its point compressed into a single sentence:

I have some new arrivals in the city who I think will interest you if you can spare the time for a visit.

Hornblower sighed; his report to London would never be finished, apparently, but he could not ignore this invitation.

'Call away my barge,' he said to the midshipman, and turned to lock his desk.

God knew who these 'new arrivals' would be. As his barge danced over the water he looked over at the siege-lines; the battering guns were still volleying away—he had grown so used to the noise that he only noticed it when his attention was called to it—and the usual long pall of smoke lay over the flat country there.

Then the boat entered the mouth of the river and Daugavgriva's ruins were hidden from view save for the dome of the church where he had so often stood. Riga came steadily nearer and nearer, and they had to keep close to the bank to avoid the worst of the Dwina's rapid current, until at last the oars ceased and the barge slid against the steps of the river-wall. At the head of them waited the Governor with his staff and a spare horse for Hornblower.

'It is only a short ride,' said Essen, 'and one I think you will consider worth the making.'

Hornblower climbed on to his horse, with a nod of thanks to the groom who held its head, and then they all wheeled and dashed away through the clattering streets. A postern was opened for them in the eastern fortifications—so far no enemy had shown his face on this bank of the Dwina—and they rode out over a drawbridge spanning the ditch. On the glacis beyond the ditch was a large force of soldiers, squatting and lying in rank; as soon as the cavalcade appeared they came hastily to their feet, dressed their lines, and then, in obedience to a shrill chorus of bugles, presented arms, their regimental colours fluttering in the little breeze. Essen reined up, returning the salute.

'Well, what do you think of them, sir?' he asked Hornblower with a chuckle.

They were ragged soldiers—bare skin showed frequently in the ranks through holes in the blue or dirty grey uniforms. They were shambling, unsoldierly soldiers, too; any troops who had seen hard service might be ragged, but Hornblower, looking along the ranks, had the impression of voluntary dirt and disorder. There were several thousand men, a strong brigade or a weak division; Hornblower glanced at the regimental standards to ascertain the number of units present, and then he nearly lost his precarious seat with surprise. Those flags were red and yellow, the national colours of Spain, and the moment this dawned upon him he realized that the ragged uniforms were the remains of the Bourbon white and blue he had come so much to hate ten years ago during his captivity at Ferrol. Not only that, but on the left of the line there was a single standard of silver and blue—the Portuguese flag, held aloft before a single shrunken battalion of scarecrows.

'I thought you would be surprised, sir,' said Essen, still chuckling.'

'Who are these men?' asked Hornblower.

'Some of Bonaparte's willing allies,' replied Essen, ironically. 'They were in St Cyr's Corps at Polotsk. One day they found themselves on the very fringe of the outpost line, and fought their way down the river to join us. Come and meet their general.'

He urged his horse forward, and he and Hornblower cantered up to where a ragged officer sat a bony white horse at the head of an even worse-mounted staff.

'I have the honour to present,' said Essen, formally, 'His Excellency the Conde de los Altos—His Excellency Commodore Sir Horatio Hornblower.'

The Conde saluted; it took Hornblower a few moments to make himself think in Spanish—the last time he had used that language was during the abortive attack on Rosas, two years ago.

'It is highly gratifying to meet Your Excellency,' he said.

The Conde's expression revealed his startled pleasure at being addressed in his own tongue, and he replied rapidly:

'You are the English Admiral, sir?'

Hornblower did not see fit to enter into explanations regarding the difference between an Admiral and a Commodore. He merely nodded.

'I have asked that my men and the Portuguese be returned by sea to Spain, there to fight against Bonaparte on our own soil. They tell me that as this can only be done by sea your consent must be secured. You will grant it, of course, sir?'

That was asking a good deal. Five thousand men at four tons a man meant twenty thousand tons of shipping—a large convoy; it would be straining his powers for him to pledge his government to provide twenty thousand tons of shipping to carry the Spaniards from Riga to Spain. There never were enough ships. On the other hand five thousand men would make a considerable army in Spain—where the Spaniards were likely to do their best—while it was only a trifling force in this continental war of millions. But none of this was of nearly as much importance as the moral side. What would be the effect on the other unwilling allies of Bonaparte, the Prussians and the Austrians, the Bavarians and the Italians, when they heard not merely that a national contingent had fought its way to join the allies, but had been received with open arms, fêted and made much of, and finally shipped back to their native land with the least possible delay? This might be the beginning of the crumbling of Bonaparte's Empire.

'I shall be very happy to send you and your men to Spain as quickly as it can be arranged,' he said. 'I will issue orders to-day for shipping to be collected.'

The Conde was profuse in his thanks, but Hornblower had something to add.

'There is one thing I ask in return,' he said, and the Conde's countenance fell a little.

'What is it, sir?' he asked.

'Your signature to a proclamation, that is all. I shall endeavour to circulate among Bonaparte's other forced allies the news of your joining the cause of liberty, and I would like you to attest its truth.'

The Conde darted one more keen look at Hornblower before he agreed.

'I will sign it,' he said.

That immediate consent was a pretty compliment, first to Hornblower's obvious honesty of purpose, and second to the reputation the Navy had acquired of always fulfilling its engagements.

'There is nothing more to be done, then,' said Hornblower, 'save to draw up the proclamation and to find ships for your forces.'

Essen was fidgeting in his saddle beside them while this conversation was going on in Spanish; he clearly knew no word of that language and was restless in consequence.

'Has he told you about conditions in Bonaparte's army?' asked Essen. 'Have you heard about the hunger and the disease?'

'Not yet,' said Hornblower.

The story came out rapidly, staccato, drawn from the Conde's lips by explosive promptings from Essen. Bonaparte's army had been dying on its feet long before it reached Moscow; hunger and disease had thinned its ranks as Bonaparte hurried it by forced marches across the desolated plains.

'The horses are nearly all dead already. There was only green rye to give them,' said the Conde.

An orderly officer was galloping madly towards them, the dust flying from beneath the ringing hoofs of his charger. He reined up before Essen with a perfunctory salute, the words of his message pouring from his lips before his hand had left his forehead. A word from the Governor sent him flying back whence he came, and Essen turned to Hornblower.

'The enemy is massing in his trenches,' he said. 'They are about to assault Daugravgriva.'

Essen began blaring orders to his staff; horses wheeled and pranced as spurs were struck into their sides and the cruel bits dragged their heads round. In a moment half a dozen officers were galloping in different directions with the messages flung at them.

'I'm going there,' said Essen.

'I shall come too,' said Hornblower.

Hornblower found it hard to stay in the saddle as his excited horse swung round beside the Governor's; he had to resettle himself, his hand on the pommel, and regain his lost stirrup as they clattered along. He was conscious of the swirling water of the Dwina as they crossed the bridge, and then on his right hand as they galloped along the quays. The roar of the bombardment grew louder and louder, and then suddenly died away.

'It is the moment of the assault!' bellowed Essen, bending

his clumsy body forward in an effort to get more speed out of his labouring horse.

Now they were in the village itself, among the ruins of the cottages, and here they met broken troops, stumbling back pell-mell, blue uniforms grey with dust, with cursing officers trying to rally them, and beating the stupefied men with the flats of their swords. Essen's voice blared out again, like a tuneless trumpet; he was waving his sword over his head and spurring forward into the press. At the sight of him the men began to rally, turning back to face the enemy, and instinctively closing together into line.

Down through the ruins came a disordered column of the enemy—it must have come up over the breach like a whirlwind. By now it was more of a mob than a column, officers capering at the head of their men, waving their hats and swords. A standard waved over them. The appearance of a formed line caused a momentary hesitation, and ragged firing broke out on both sides; Hornblower saw one of the capering officers fall dead as he called to his men to come on. He looked over at Essen, but he was still towering high in the smoke. Hornblower wheeled his horse towards the flank; his mind was working with the ecstatic speed of excitement, bullets were singing by him, and he knew that this was the crisis of the assault. Halt an attacking column for one moment, and then any trifle might turn the scale, and it would go back as fast as it had advanced. He reached the door of the church just as a flood of men came pouring out of it—the garrison of the building hastening to make good their retreat before they should be cut off and isolated. Hornblower tore his sword from its sheath, miraculously retaining his seat in the saddle.

'Come on!' he yelled, waving the weapon.

They did not understand his words, as they blinked at this vision in blue and gold before them, but anyone could understand his gestures. At the back of the group Hornblower caught a momentary glimpse of Clausewitz and Diebitch, who should have taken command here, but there was no time for argument, and racing through Hornblower's brain went the conviction at the same time that although they might be scientific soldiers they would be useless in a physical rough-and-tumble like this.

'Come on!' yelled Hornblower again, pointing with his sword at the flank of the assaulting column.

They turned to follow him—no one could have resisted the inspiration of his example and gestures. Column and line were still exchanging ragged volleys, the column still moving forward little by little, the line wavering and falling back.

'Form line!' yelled Hornblower, turning in his saddle, his spread arms and gesticulating fists telling the Russians what he wanted them to do. 'Load your muskets!'

They formed their line, marching up after him, hands busy with their ramrods—a couple of hundred men at most, jostling each other as they stumbled over the ruins of the cottages. Now they were right on the flank of the column; Hornblower saw faces turn towards them. He was even near enough to see surprise and dismay in the attitudes of the men who suddenly realized that a new force was about to assail their flank.

'Fire!' yelled Hornblower, and some sort of volley crashed out from the ragged line he led.

He saw two ramrods sail forward in soaring arcs, fired out of their muskets by excited men who had been caught in the act of loading by his order, and who had incontinently put their weapons to their shoulders and pulled their triggers. One ramrod buried itself like an arrow in the body of a French soldier. The column wavered and staggered—not one man in

a hundred there had expected this attack on the flank; all
their attention had been taken up by Essen's line in front of
them.

'Charge!' yelled Hornblower, waving his sword and urging
his horse forward.

The Russians followed him with a cheer; the whole column
of the enemy, Hornblower saw, was wavering and melting
away, the disordered ranks crumbling. They were turning
their backs, and the memory streaked through his excited
mind of a saying he had heard somewhere to the effect that
the knapsacks of the enemy were the most cheering sight a
soldier could behold. Then he saw one of the enemy swing
back again and level his musket at him. As the smoke gushed
from the barrel his horse gave a convulsive leap and then put
his nose to the ground and somersaulted; for a moment
Hornblower felt himself flying through the air; he was too
excited and exalted to feel any fear, so that the crash with
which he hit the earth came as a startling surprise to him.
But even though the breath was dashed from his body and the
jar shook every bone in it, his fantastic mind still thought
clearly, and he heard and felt the flank attack which he had
led sweep cheering over him. Only when he rose to his feet
did he come to the sudden realization that he was bruised and
weak, so that it was hard to balance on his legs—they nearly
gave way under him as he hobbled forward to pick up his
sword which lay shining on the dusty earth between two dead
men.

He felt suddenly alone, but the feeling had hardly time to
take hold of him when he was engulfed in a wave of humanity,
Essen and his staff roaring with exaltation and delight. He
stood there, bruised and torn, his sword dangling from his
hand, as they overwhelmed him with incomprehensible con-
gratulations. One of the officers leaped down from his horse,

'Charge!' yelled Hornblower

and Hornblower was hauled and pushed up into the saddle, and they cantered forward, the horses picking their way delicately over the dead and wounded, over the tortured ground, towards the ramparts. The last remnants of the assaulting forces were being driven back through the breach to the accompaniment of a straggling musketry fire. As they neared the fortifications the guns of the foiled besiegers reopened fire, and a shot or two came howling overhead. Essen reined up, like a sensible man, and then walked his horse out of the line of fire.

'That was a moment to remember,' he said, looking round at the area where the clash had occurred.

Hornblower's head was still clear. He realized what a bitter blow this reverse must be to the besiegers. After all the fierce preliminary fighting they had sapped up to the ramparts, made their breach, and launched the assault which should have captured the place, only to be flung back when the breach was in their hands. He knew that Macdonald would have the greatest difficulty in inducing his men to assault again— a bloody failure like this would make them turn sulky and grudging of their lives. Certainly Macdonald would have to allow a considerable time to elapse, and would have to continue his battering for several more days, and multiply his approaches and parallels, before he could risk another assault. Maybe the town would hold. Maybe that attack would be the last. Hornblower felt prophetic, inspired. He remembered how he had heard the news of Masséna's retreat from before Lisbon—that had been the first of the ebb of the Empire in the South, and now Wellington was in Madrid and threatening France. Maybe Riga would mark the limits of the Empire in the North. Maybe that penetration through the breach would be remembered as the farthest north Bonaparte's men would ever attain. At that rate—Hornblower's

pulse beat quicker—the flank attack he had led, that un-
foreseen charge of a couple of hundred men hurriedly
gathered up in the tumult, had been the blow which had
thwarted Bonaparte's schemes to conquer the world. That
was what he had done. And it would look extraordinarily well
in *The Times* that 'Commodore Sir Horatio Hornblower, K.B.,
had his horse killed under him while leading a charge.'

Exultation and inspiration ended abruptly, and Hornblower felt suddenly weak and ill. He knew that if he did not
dismount quickly he would fall from his saddle. He took hold
of the pommel and kicked his right foot clear of the stirrup,
swung his leg over, and then as his feet touched ground the
ground came up to meet him. He only recovered some indefi-
nite number of minutes later, to find himself seated on the
ground, his stock unbuckled, and his face clammy with cold
sweat. Essen was bending anxiously over him, and someone,
apparently a surgeon, was kneeling at his side.

Then Brown appeared, cutlass at his side and pistols in
his belt, followed by other members of the barge's crew.
Apparently he had seen his captain ride over the bridge, and,
like the good subordinate he was, had brought the boat across
after him. Brown's face was contorted with anxiety, and he
threw himself, too, on his knees beside Hornblower.

'Wounded, sir? Where is it? Can I——'

'No, no, no,' said Hornblower pettishly, pushing Brown
away and getting to his feet, swaying. 'It's nothing.'

It was extraordinarily maddening to see a look of admira-
tion come over Brown's face. Anyone would think he was
being heroic instead of merely sensible. Not far away—at the
foot of the breach, apparently—a trumpet was pealing, high
challenging notes, and this served to distract the crowd from
their solicitude. Everyone looked in the direction of the
sound, and presently a group of Russian officers approached

them, leading a blindfold figure dressed in the blue trimmed with grey astrakhan of the French Imperial Staff. A word from Essen removed the bandage, and the officer—he wore a grey Hussar moustache—saluted with dignity.

'The chef d'escadron Verrier,' he said, 'aide-de-camp to Marshal Macdonald. I am ordered by the Marshal to suggest a suspension of hostilities for two hours. The breach is covered with the wounded of both sides, and it would be only humane to remove them. Each side can remove its own.'

'There are more French and German wounded than Russian, I am sure,' said Essen, in his horrible French.

'French or Russian, sir,' said the parlementaire, 'they will die unless they receive speedy aid.'

Hornblower's mind was beginning to work again. Ideas were leaping to the surface like wreckage from a sunken ship. He caught Essen's eye and nodded meaningly, and Essen, like a good diplomatist, gave no sign of having received the hint as he shifted his glance back to Verrier.

'The request is granted, sir,' he said, 'in the name of humanity.'

'I thank Your Excellency, in the name of humanity,' said Verrier, saluting, and then looking round for someone to blindfold him again and lead him through the breach.

The moment he was gone Hornblower turned to Brown.

'Take the barge back to the ship,' he ordered. 'Hurry. My compliments to Captain Bush, and I would like you to bring back Lieutenant von Bulow to me. One of the lieutenants of equal rank will have to accompany him. Hurry!'

'Aye aye, sir.'

That was all that was necessary with Brown or Bush, thank God. A simple order brought simple yet intelligent obedience. Hornblower saluted Essen.

'Would it be possible, Your Excellency,' he asked, 'to

bring the Spanish troops over to this side of the river? I have a German prisoner whom I am going to return to the enemy, and I should like him to see the Spaniards with his own eyes first.'

Essen grinned with blubber lips.

'I do my best not merely to comply with every one of your wishes, sir, but even to anticipate them. The last order I gave on the other side of the river was for the Spaniards to be brought over—they were the nearest formed troops and I intended to use them as garrison for the warehouses on the quay. I have no doubt they are there already. You would like them marched in this direction?'

'If you would be so kind, sir.'

Hornblower was casually waiting for nothing in particular at the jetty when the boat touched at it, and Lieutenant von Bulow, of the Fifty-first Regiment of Prussian Infantry, stepped ashore under the escort of Mr Tooth and Brown and his men.

'There is an armistice at the moment,' explained Hornblower, 'between your army and ours. No, it is not peace—merely to clear the wounded from the breach. But I was going to take this opportunity of returning you to your friends. Naturally, you have not been properly exchanged, but you can, if you wish, give me your word that you will not serve against His Britannic Majesty nor against His Imperial Russian Majesty until an exchange has been effected.'

'I give you my word,' said Bulow, after a moment's thought.

'Excellent! Then perhaps I might give myself the pleasure of walking with you as far as the breach?'

As they left the jetty and began the brief walk through the ruins of the village Bulow was darting the quick glances of a professional soldier about him. Hornblower made polite conversation as they strolled.

At the foot of the church tower there was a Spanish regiment, the men lying down in their ranks. At the sight of Hornblower the colonel called his men to their feet and saluted. Hornblower returned the salute, conscious as he did so that Bulow at his side had not failed to notice the troops. His eyes were bulging with unasked questions.

'Spanish troops,' said Hornblower, casually. 'A division of Spaniards and Portuguese joined us from Bonaparte's main army a little while ago. They fight well—in fact they were responsible for the final repulse of the last assault. It is interesting to notice how Bonaparte's dupes are falling away from him now that the hollowness of his power is revealed.'

Bulow's astonished reply must either have been inarticulate or in German, for Hornblower could not understand it, but his tone conveyed his meaning well enough.

'It goes without saying,' said Hornblower casually, 'that I would like to see the magnificent Prussian Army ranged among Bonaparte's enemies and England's allies, too. But naturally your King knows his own policy best—unless, of course, surrounded as he is by Bonaparte's men, he is not free to choose.'

Bulow stared at him in amazement; Hornblower was putting forward a viewpoint which was quite new to him, but Hornblower still made himself talk with the utmost casualness, as if he were doing no more than making polite conversation.

'That's high politics,' he said with a laugh and a wave of his hand. 'But one day in the future we might look back on this conversation as prophetic. One cannot tell, can one? Some time when we meet as plenipotentiaries I will be able to remind you of this talk. And here we are at the breach. It irks me to have to say good-bye, at the same moment as it gives me pleasure to restore you to your friends. My heartiest good wishes, sir, for you for the future.'

Bulow saluted stiffly again, and then, as Hornblower held out his hand, shook hands with him. To the Prussian it was a remarkable occurrence, for a Commodore to condescend to shake hands with a mere subaltern.

Raising the Siege

THE new problem which Hornblower was debating as he walked his quarter-deck, while H.M.S. *Nonsuch* swung at anchor in Riga Bay, was one which he had long foreseen, but which lost none of its urgency for all that. Here was winter coming; the days were growing short and the nights long, and the brackish water of Riga Bay was covered with a thin scum of ice. If he stayed much longer his ships would be frozen in. Prudence dictated an immediate withdrawal.

And yet he could not withdraw. When he had mentioned the possibility Essen had shown positive dismay. If his men were to see the British ships go away they would be quite sure the place was doomed. The British naval officer who had led the final charge at Daugavgriva had grown into a legendary figure in their minds, a mascot, a symbol of good luck. If he were to leave them that would be a proof, in the men's minds, that he had lost hope. He could not possibly withdraw.

Here was a fool of a midshipman in his way dodging about in front of him as though bent on distracting him from his train of thought.

'B-b-boat approaching, sir,' stammered the youth. 'M-Mr Hurst told me to tell you. He thinks the Governor's on board.'

'Why wasn't I told before?' said Hornblower. He strode to the side. The Governor was approaching in a big pulling-boat, which was steering towards them along the clear

channel through the thin ice which the last eddies of the
Dwina river still kept clear before they lost themselves in the
Bay. As the Governor caught sight of him he sprang up into
the sternsheets waving his cocked hat, he even tried to dance,
precariously, both arms extended over his head, at imminent
risk of falling overboard.

'Something's up, sir,' said Bush at Hornblower's side.

'That looks like good news,' said Hornblower.

The Governor arrived on the quarter-deck, hat still in hand.
He flung his arms round Hornblower and hugged him, swinging his lean body up into the air so that his feet left the deck.
Hornblower could imagine the grins that were being exchanged around him as he kicked in the air like a baby. The
Governor put him down, clapped his hat on his head, and
then seized first Hornblower's hand and then Bush's, and
tried to dance a sort of ring-a-ring-of-roses with the two
Englishmen. There was no more controlling him than one
could control a bear.

'What is the news, Your Excellency?' asked Hornblower;
Essen's grip on his hand was painful.

'Oh,' said Essen, flinging the Englishman's hands away so
as to spread his arms again. 'Bonaparte has started to retreat.'

'Has he, by God!' said Hornblower.

'He left Moscow five days back,' roared Essen. 'We beat
him at Malo-Jaroslavetz. Beat him in a pitched battle, and
now he's running as hard as he can for Smolensk and Warsaw.
And he won't get there before the snows! He'll be lucky if
he gets there at all! Chichagov is marching hard to cut off
his retreat at the Beresina. He's ruined. They're dying in
thousands every night already! Nothing to eat, and winter's
here!'

Essen stamped grotesquely about the deck, more like a
dancing bear than ever.

'Please, sir, *please*. What does he say?' asked Bush
pathetically.

Hornblower translated to the best of his ability, the other
quarter-deck officers eavesdropping shamelessly.

'We can get out of this bay before the ice comes, by God!'
said Bush, snapping his fingers; it was obvious that if he had
not a wooden leg he would be dancing too.

Hornblower looked across at the mainland.

'Macdonald's shown no sign of retreating yet,' he said. 'If
he had the Governor would have mentioned it.'

'But don't you think he'll have to, sir?' Bush's expressive
face showed anxiety now instead of joy.

'He may have to retreat,' said Hornblower, 'but until then
we stay here, unless I receive orders to the contrary.'

Essen caught sight of their sober faces and turned on them
again. He slapped Bush on the back so that he staggered with
the force of the blow; he snapped his fingers under Hornblower's nose, and pirouetted with the grace of a performing
seal. It was absurd that with all this going on, with Bush
asking questions regarding the future, with Essen acting like
a lunatic, Hornblower's brain should be planning and thinking still, with that swift clarity and that fevered rapidity
which he knew by now portended some new development.
Bonaparte in retreat, Bonaparte beaten, meant a tremendous
revulsion of feeling throughout Europe. All the world knew
that Wellington was threatening France from the south; and
now the Empire was in peril from the east. The King of
Prussia was practically a prisoner in French hands, but the
Prussian army—the greater part of the force now besieging
Riga—could act as a free agent if it wished. The desertion
of the Spaniards had shown them the way, and the pamphlets
which he had had printed in Riga and distributed among the
besiegers by Russian pedlars would not let them forget the

lesson. Bulow would be able to bear witness to the truth of his assertions—Hornblower was glad he had set him free.

'I am sending Diebitch out to beat up the besiegers' lines with a sally,' Essen was saying. 'I must see how *they* take this news. Would you care to accompany me, sir?'

'Of course,' said Hornblower, coming out abruptly from his dreaming. What with fatigue—he was always weary now —and rapid thinking and excitement he was still a little 'mazy,' as they said of fuddled men in the village when he was a boy. He announced his departure to Bush.

'You're worn out, sir,' protested Bush. 'You're no more than a shadow. Send someone else, sir. Send me. Send Duncan. You've done all that's necessary, sir.'

'I haven't yet,' said Hornblower, but he stooped so far as to risk delay by offering Essen refreshment, with the suggestion that they should drink a toast to celebrate this glorious news.

'Thank you, no,' said Essen, to Hornblower's relief. 'Diebitch will attack at dusk, and the days are short now.'

'You'll take your barge, sir, won't you?' persisted Bush. 'Take Brown.'

Bush was like a fussy parent with a venturesome child— like a hen with one chick. He was always nervous about entrusting his precious Hornblower to these unpredictable Russians; Hornblower grinned at Bush's solicitude.

'Anything to keep you happy,' he said.

Hornblower's barge followed the Governor's pulling-boat along the channel through the ice; Hornblower sat with the Governor in the stern of the Russian boat. There was a chill wind blowing, and the skies were grey.

'We shall have more snow,' said Essen, looking up at the clouds. 'God help the French.'

In the absence of any sunshine there was a mortal chill

in the air. Hornblower thought of the French marching over the desolate plains of Russia, and was sorry for them. And the snow came indeed, that afternoon, sweeping over river and village, making white innocuous mounds of the battered parapets and the shattered guns and the graves which were scattered through the village. It was already prematurely dark when the ever-patient Russian grenadiers lined the trenches and then sallied forth upon the enemy's lines. They were not more than half-way across no-man's-land before the guns began to fire upon them, stabbing the falling snow with their bright orange flashes.

'No sign of any retreat there,' was Clausewitz's comment as he watched the fierce struggle from the gallery of the church beside Essen and Hornblower.

And if confirmation was needed the attacking party could supply it when it came drifting back in the darkness, decimated. The besiegers had met their sally with spirit; they had had patrols out in no-man's-land, and the trenches were adequately guarded. In retaliation, the besiegers opened fire with their breaching batteries; the ground shook to the rumble of the discharges, and the black night was stabbed again by the flames of the guns. It was impossible to maintain good aim or elevation in the darkness; it was only a short time before the shots were flying wild, all over the village, so that the defenders as far back as the Dwina river had to keep low in their trenches.

Immediately under Hornblower's gaze there was a battery of four heavy pieces, firing regular salvoes at short intervals. He noted the four bursts of flame over and over again, so that when there was a longer interval he was surprised first by the absence of sound and then by its unexpected coming. The flashes endured their brief moment, to be succeeded again by night, but Hornblower found himself wondering what difference there had been between this salvo and the last, apart from the longer interval which had preceded it. One flash—the right-hand one—had not been as distinct as the other three, longer and yet intense. Some error in loading, perhaps. Then came the next salvo, and only three flashes; the right-hand gun had not fired. Maybe it had 'unbushed' itself—blown out its vent fitting, as guns sometimes did. Another long interval, and then another salvo—two sharp flashes, and one longer one. The next salvo only two guns fired, and Hornblower realized what had been going on. He plucked at Essen's sleeve.

'They are destroying their guns over there,' he said. 'They are firing some shots at us while at each salvo they fire a shot against the trunnions of one of the guns. There were four guns over there, Your Excellency. Now—see—there are only two.'

'Possibly,' admitted Essen, staring into the darkness.

'The firing is dying away,' agreed Clausewitz, 'but perhaps they are only growing tired of wasting ammunition.'

There was only one flash from the battery next time, and there was something clearly odd about it.

'The last gun in the battery,' commented Essen. 'Probably they have burst it by overloading.'

He trained his telescope in the darkness.

'Look over there at their main camps,' he added. 'Watch those fires. They seem to be burning brightly, but——'

Hornblower directed his gaze to the distant rows of campfires, sparkling very dimly in the thick night. He looked backwards and forwards along one of the rows, trying to keep track of them all. He thought he saw one fire wink and go out, but he could not be sure. His eyes were watering with the cold and with the strain, and as he rubbed them Essen shut his telescope with a snap.

'They are dying down,' he said. 'I'm sure of it, and no troops would allow their camp-fires to die down on a night like this. Clausewitz, get your men ready to attack again. Diebitch——'

The Governor began rapping out orders. Hornblower had a momentary feeling of pity for the Russian soldiers, huddled in their freezing trenches, dispirited by their recent repulse and losses, now ordered to go out again to what would seem to them to be certain disaster in the night. The wind suddenly shrieked down upon them, piercing him to the bone, despite the cloak he clutched round himself.

' 'Ere you are, sir,' said Brown's voice unexpectedly in his ear. 'I've brought you up a blanket. Let's put it round you under your cloak. And 'ere's your gloves, sir.'

Deftly in the darkness Brown draped the blanket over him, so that his cloak held it down over his shoulders. It would look fantastic in daylight, but fortunately it was still dark. Hornblower was shivering, and he stamped his frozen feet in an endeavour to warm them.

'Aren't those men of yours ever going to attack Clausewitz?' grumbled Essen. 'What's the time? One o'clock? Send down to your brigadier and tell him I'll have him cashiered if he does not pull his men together for an immediate advance.'

There was a long freezing interval, before the darkness before them was pricked by a few little pin-points of flame— musket shots in the second parallel.

'Ha!' said Essen.

There was another long wait before the message came back. The sortie had found the advanced trenches abandoned save for a few posts. They were pushing forward now through the snow and the darkness towards the main camp.

'They're going, then,' said Essen. 'Have the cavalry

paraded two hours before dawn. I'll catch their rear-guard at daylight. I want all troops across the river then. And now a glass of tea, for the love of God.'

Warming himself at the fire burning on the flagged floor of the church, drinking hot tea through his chattering teeth, Hornblower looked round at these men of iron who showed no sign of fatigue and hardly any of cold. He himself was too chilled, and, oddly, too fatigued, to gain much benefit from the chance of resting for a couple of hours on the trusses of straw laid out beside the high altar, but Essen snored volcanically until the moment when his aide-de-camp shook him awake. Outside it was still dark, and colder than ever, when the horses were brought up to the church door for them to mount.

'I better come with you, sir,' said Brown. 'I got myself a 'orse.'

How Brown had done that Hornblower could not imagine, seeing the difficulties of language. The cavalcade moved slowly in the darkness towards the Mitau suburb, the horses slipping and stumbling in the snow; Hornblower found himself wishing he had been able to retain his blanket when he mounted, for it was colder than ever in the faint grey light. Suddenly from far ahead of them came a sullen flat thud, and another, and another—field-guns firing a long way off.

'Diebitch is up to their rear-guard,' said Essen. 'Good!'

There was enough light now to reveal the desolation of their surroundings as they approached the deserted siege-works. They could look down into the littered trenches; there were the batteries, with the shattered siege-guns standing drunkenly at the embrasures, and here was a dead horse, lying on its back, its belly shrouded with snow, out of which its legs pointed stiffly at the grey sky. And here was the main camp, rows and rows of little huts; mostly only two or three feet high, with the dead remains of camp fires already buried in snow.

When at last they reached the point where the track joined the high road the signs of real fighting began; dead and wounded soldiers, Russian, French, and German, where the Russian advance-guard had clashed with the rear-guard. Then they caught up with the Russian columns plodding sturdily up the road, and trotted past their interminable length, one division and then another; the men were silent with the exertion of stepping out as fast as their legs would carry them under their heavy knapsacks, and this ten miles of fast marching had greatly modified the first jubilation of pursuit.

'Macdonald has made a good retreat,' said Clausewitz, 'at the cost of leaving his sick and his guns behind. I wonder how long he will be able to keep this pace up?'

Hornblower did not trouble to enter into the discussion. Saddle soreness was making him abstracted, apart from his fatigue and his general feeling of malaise. But he had to be able to report to his government that he had followed up the retreating army for at least one march on its way back to Germany; it would be better if it were two or three. And there was something else. He wanted to catch up with the Prussians, even if it were the last thing he did—and it was odd that he had this feeling that it was the last thing he was ever going to do. His head was whirling, and there was something comforting about the knowledge that Brown was just back there with the mounted orderlies.

A messenger brought back news from the advance-guard, and Hornblower heard Clausewitz's explanation as if in a dream.

'The Prussians are making a stand at the fork in the roads ahead,' he said. 'They are covering the retreat while the other two army corps get away by the two roads.'

It was strange that this was just what he was expecting, as if it were a story he had already heard being retold.

'The Prussians!' he said, and without willing it he pressed his legs against his horse's sides to urge it to a faster pace towards where the flat reports of the guns showed where the Prussians were holding back the advance-guard. The headquarters party was clear of the main body now, trotting along the deeply-rutted road, hemmed in here by a dense wood of coniferous trees. Beyond the wood the desolate landscape opened up to reveal a low ridge up which the road mounted ahead of them. On either side of the road here a brigade of the Russian advance-guard was halted, a battery of artillery was in action, and up on the ridge could be seen the Prussian infantry columns, black blocks against grey fields. Over on the right a grey-clad Russian column was plodding across country to turn the flank of the position, while between the two forces Russian horsemen—Cossacks—trotted in ones and twos on their shaggy ponies, their long lances vertical at their sides. A watery sun broke through the clouds at this moment, seeming merely to accentuate the gloominess of the landscape. A general came up to salute Essen, but Hornblower did not want to listen to what he had to say. He wanted to press forward towards the Prussians, and as the horses of the party followed the example of his own they moved steadily up the road, Essen half unconscious of the movements of his horse as he listened to the general's report. He was only recalled to his surroundings by the howl of a cannon-shot which pitched at the roadside near him, throwing snow and earth in all directions.

'What do we think we're doing?' he asked. 'We'll be getting ourselves shot in a moment.'

Hornblower was staring forward at the Prussian army, at the glitter of bayonets and the flags black against the snow.

'I want to go up to the Prussians,' he said.

The discharge of the battery close at hand drowned the words Essen said in reply, but what he meant to say was plain enough.

'I am going,' said Hornblower stubbornly. He looked round and caught Clausewitz's eye. 'Are you coming too, Colonel?'

'Of course he cannot,' expostulated Essen. 'He cannot risk being taken.'

As a renegade, a man fighting against his own country, Clausewitz was likely to be hanged if ever the Prussians laid hands on him.

'It would be better if he came,' said Hornblower, woodenly. This was a strange feeling of simultaneous clairvoyance and illness.

'I'll go with the Commodore,' said Clausewitz suddenly, making what was probably the bravest decision of his life. Perhaps he was carried away by Hornblower's automaton-like recklessness.

Essen shrugged his shoulders at this madness which had descended upon them.

'Go, then,' he said. 'Perhaps I may be able to capture enough generals to exchange for you.'

They trotted forward up the road; Hornblower heard Essen bellow an order to the battery commander to cease fire. He looked back; Brown was trotting after them, a respectful five lengths behind. They passed close to some of the Cossack light horse, who looked at them curiously, and then they were in among Prussian skirmishers, who, from the shelter of bushes and inequalities in the ground, were taking long shots at the Cossacks. No one fired at them as they rode boldly through. A Prussian captain beside the road saluted them, and Clausewitz returned the salute. Just beyond the skirmishing line was the first formed infantry, a Prussian regiment in battalion columns of companies, two on one side of the road and one on the other. The colonel and his staff were standing in the road staring at the odd trio approaching them—the British naval officer in his blue and gold, Clausewitz in his Russian uniform with the row of medals, and the British seaman with cutlass and pistols at his belt. The colonel asked a question in a loud dry tone as they approached, and Clausewitz answered it, reining in.

'Tell them we must see the general,' said Hornblower in French to Clausewitz.

There was a rapid exchange of dialogue between Clausewitz and the colonel, ending in the latter calling up two or three mounted officers—his adjutant and majors, perhaps— to accompany them up the road. Here they saw a larger infantry force formed up, and a line of guns, and here was a party on horseback, the feathers and braid and medals and mounted orderlies indicating the presence of a general's staff. This must be the general—Yorck, Hornblower remembered his name to be. He recognized Clausewitz at once, and addressed him abruptly in German. A few words on each side seemed only to add to the tension of the situation, and there was a short pause.

'He speaks French,' said Clausewitz to Hornblower, and they both turned and waited for him to speak.

'General,' said Hornblower; he was in a dream, but he made himself speak in his dream. 'I represent the King of England, and Colonel Clausewitz represents the Emperor of Russia. We are fighting to free Europe from Bonaparte. Are you fighting to maintain him as a tyrant?'

It was a rhetorical question to which no answer was possible. Silent perforce, Yorck could only await the rest of what Hornblower had to say.

'Bonaparte is beaten. He is retreating from Moscow, and not ten thousand of his army will reach Germany. The Spaniards have deserted him, as you know. So have the Portuguese. All Europe is turning upon him, having found out how little his promises mean. You know of his treatment of Germany—I need not tell you about that. If you fight for him you may keep him on his tottering throne for a few days longer. You may drag out Germany's agony by that length of time. But your duty is to your enslaved country, to your King who is a prisoner. You can free them. You can end the useless pouring-out of the blood of your men now, at this moment.'

Yorck looked away from him, over the bleak countryside, at the Russian army slowly deploying, before he replied.

'What do you suggest?' he said.

That was all Hornblower wanted to hear. If Yorck was willing to ask questions, instead of immediately making prisoners of them, the matter was as good as settled. He could leave the discussion to Clausewitz, and sink back into the weariness which was rising round him like a tide. He brought Clausewitz into the conversation with a glance.

'An armistice,' said Clausewitz. 'An immediate suspension of hostilities. The definitive terms can be settled easily enough at leisure.'

Yorck still hesitated for a moment. Hornblower, despite his weariness and illness, could study him with a renewed flicker of interest; the hard face, sunburned to mahogany, the white hair and moustache in strange contrast. Yorck was on the edge of his fate. At present he was a loyal subject of the King of Prussia, a comparatively undistinguished general. He had only to say two words, and they would make him a traitor now and conceivably an historic figure in the future. Prussia's defection—at any rate, the defection of the Prussian army—would reveal the hollowness of the Napoleonic Empire in a way nothing else could do. It rested with Yorck.

'I agree,' said Yorck.

That was all Hornblower wanted to hear. He could lapse into his dream—his nightmare—now, let the rest of the discussion take whatever course it would. When Clausewitz turned back down the road Hornblower's horse followed him without any guidance from Hornblower. Brown appeared, just his face; there was nothing else that Hornblower could see.

News of Mutiny

The fatigue and weakness from which Hornblower had been suffering during the last days of the siege of Riga were the early symptoms of the Russian typhus with which he collapsed completely as soon as he had achieved his purpose with General Yorck. He was sent back to England immediately and was slowly nursed back to health after a year of convalescence at his home in the village of Smallbridge in Kent.

THE chapel stall of carved oak on which Sir Horatio Hornblower was sitting was most uncomfortable, and the sermon which the Dean of Westminster was preaching was deadly dull. Hornblower fidgeted like a child, and like a child he peered round the chapel and at the congregation to distract his mind from his physical troubles.

118

This was the price he had to pay for having a ribbon and star to wear, for being a Knight of the Most Honourable Order of the Bath; as he was known to be on sick leave in England—and fully convalescent—he could not possibly evade attendance at this, the most important ceremonial of the Order. Certainly the chapel looked effective enough, the dull sunshine which made its way through the windows being reflected and multiplied into a soul-stirring glow by the knights' crimson mantles and flashing orders. The important-looking person over there with a silver gilt crown on his head and velvet tabard embroidered in the royal arms was merely Bath King-at-Arms. Beside him was the Prince Regent, the Sovereign of the Order, his scarlet face at odds with the crimson of his mantle. And there were soldiers, generals and colonels, with whose faces he was unfamiliar. But elsewhere in the chapel there were men with whom he was proud to share the brotherhood of the Order—Lord St Vincent, huge and grim, the man who took his fleet down into the heart of a Spanish squadron twice its strength; Duncan, who destroyed the Dutch Navy at Camperdown; and a dozen more of admirals and captains, some of them even junior to him in the Navy List—Lydiard, who captured the *Pomona* off Havannah; Samuel Hood, who commanded the *Zealous* at the Nile; and Yeo, who stormed the fort at El Muro.

A uniformed naval lieutenant had made his way into the chapel, and stood hesitating for a moment before discovering Lord St Vincent and hastening to him, offering him the large despatch which he held in his hand. No one was paying any attention to the sermon now—the cream of the Royal Navy were all craning round, peering at St Vincent as he read the despatch, which had clearly arrived from the Admiralty at the other end of Whitehall. The Dean's voice wavered, and then he rallied gamely, droning on to deaf ears, and ears which remained deaf for a long time, for St Vincent, having read the despatch through once without any change of expression in his craggy face, immediately turned back to the beginning and read it through again. St Vincent who had so boldly risked the fate of England on a single prompt decision at the battle which gave him his title was nevertheless not a man to plunge hastily into action where there was time to think.

He finished his second reading, folded the despatch, and then swept his gaze round the chapel. Two score Knights of the Bath stiffened with excitement and hoped to catch his eye. St Vincent rose to his feet and clasped his crimson cloak about him; he threw a word to the waiting lieutenant, and then, seizing his plumed hat, proceeded to hobble stiffly out of the chapel. Attention immediately transferred itself to the lieutenant, who was watched by every eye as he walked across the transept, and Hornblower stirred uncomfortably, his heart beating fast, as he realized that the lieutenant was heading straight for him.

'His Lordship's compliments, sir,' said the lieutenant, 'and he would like a word with you immediately.

Now it was Hornblower's turn to fasten his mantle and to remember to pick up his plumed hat. He must at all costs appear nonchalant, and give to the assembled Knights no chance to smile at him for appearing flustered at this summons from the First Lord. He must look as if he was accustomed to this sort of thing every day. He stepped negligently out of his stall; his sword made its way between his legs and only by the mercy of Providence was he saved from tumbling headlong. He recovered himself with a clatter of spurs and scabbard, and set himself to stalk with slow dignity down the aisle.

Beyond the door St Vincent was awaiting him, the little

wind tossing the ostrich feathers of his hat and ruffling the crimson cloak of silk. His massive legs bulged the white silk trunk hose; and he was pacing up and down on huge, gouty, deformed feet that distorted the white silk shoes. But the fantastic costume in no way detracted from the grim dignity of the man.

'You're ready for active service now, Hornblower?'

'Yes, my lord.'

'You'll have to start to-night.'

'Aye aye, sir—my lord.'

'When they bring my damned coach up I'll take you to the Admiralty and give you your orders.' St Vincent lifted his voice in a bellow that had hailed the maintop in West Indian hurricanes. 'Haven't they got those damned horses in *yet*, Johnson?'

'What is the service, my lord?' asked Hornblower.

'Suppression of mutiny,' said St Vincent grimly. 'Damned bloody mutiny. It might be '94 over again. Did you ever know Chadwick—Lieutenant Augustine Chadwick?'

'Midshipman with me under Pellew, my lord.'

'Well, he's—ah, here's my damned coach at last.'

St Vincent climbed in heavily, with Hornblower beside him, and the horses' hoofs clashed on the cobbles as the heavy vehicle crawled forward. The pale sunlight flickered through the windows on St Vincent's craggy face as he sat stoop-shouldered on the leather seat; some urchins in the street caught sight of the gaily attired individuals in the coach and yelled 'Hooray,' waving their tattered caps.

'Chadwick had *Flame*, eighteen-gun brig,' said St Vincent. 'The crew's mutinied in the Bay of the Seine and are holding him and the other officers hostage. They turned a master's mate and four loyal hands adrift in the gig with an ultimatum addressed to the Admiralty. The gig made Bembridge last night, and the papers have just reached me—here they are.'

St Vincent shook in his gnarled hand the despatch and the enclosures which he had clasped since he received them in Westminster Abbey.

'What's the ultimatum, my lord?'

'Amnesty—oblivion. And hang Chadwick. Otherwise they turn the brig over to the French.'

'The crazy fools!' said Hornblower.

He could remember Chadwick in the *Indefatigable;* old for a midshipman then, twenty years ago. He must be in his fifties now, and only a lieutenant. He had been a vile-tempered midshipman; after being passed over continually for promotion he must be a worse-tempered lieutenant. He could make a little vessel like the *Flame,* in which probably he was the only commissioned officer, a perfect hell if he wanted to. That might be the basis of the mutiny. After the terrible lessons of Spithead and the Nore, after Pigott had been murdered in the *Hermione,* some of the worst characteristics of the naval service had been eliminated. It was still a hard, cruel life, but not one to drive men into the suicidal madness of mutiny unless there were some special circumstances involved. A captain both cruel and unjust, a determined and intelligent leader among the men—that combination might make a mutiny. But whatever the cause, mutiny must be suppressed instantly, visited with extreme punishment. Smallpox or the plague were no more infectious and no more fatal than mutiny in a fighting service. Allow one mutineer to escape punishment, and he would be remembered by every next man with a grievance, and his example followed.

The coach was wheeling into the Admiralty yard, and two wooden-legged naval pensioners were stumping out to open the doors. St Vincent climbed out, and he and Hornblower, in their brilliant crimson and white silk, walked through to the First Lord's room.

'There's their ultimatum,' said St Vincent, throwing a paper upon the desk.

Written in a poor hand, was Hornblower's first mental note—not the work of some bankrupt tradesman or lawyer's clerk caught by the pressgang.

> *On board H.M.S.* Flame *off Havre*
> *7th October,* 1813

> *We are all loyal hearts and true here, but Lieutenant Augustine Chadwick has flogged us and starved us, and has turned up all hands twice a watch for a month. Yesterday he said that to-day he would flog every third man of us and the rest of us as soon as the others was healed. So we have him under lock and key in his cabin, and there's a whip rove at the fore yardarm waiting for him for he ought to be strung up after what he did to the boy James Jones, he killed him and we think he said in his report that he died of fever. We want their Lordships at the Admiralty to promise us to try him for his crimes and give us new officers and let bygones be bygones. We want to fight on for England's liberties for we are loyal hearts and true like we said but France is under our lee and we are all in this together and we are not going to be hanged as mutineers and if you try to take this vessel we shall run him up to the yardarm and go in to the French. We are all signing this.*

> *Humbly and respectfully yours,*

All round the margin of the letter were the signatures, seven of them, and several score of crosses, with a note against each cross—'Henry Wilson, his mark'; 'William

Owen, his mark,' and so on; they indicated the usual proportion of literates and illiterates in an average ship's company.
Hornblower looked up at St Vincent .when he finished
examining the letter.

'Mutinous dogs,' said St Vincent.

Maybe they were, thought Hornblower. But they had a
right to be, he also thought. Faced with the certainty of a
flogging in the immediate future, they had risen in mutiny,
and he could not blame them. But it would be as well not
to let St Vincent guess at his sentiments—the First Lord
obviously hated mutineers just as mutineers, without troub-
ling to think more deeply about their case.

'What orders do you have for me, my lord?' asked
Hornblower.

'I'll give you *carte blanche*,' replied St Vincent. 'A free
hand. Bring *Flame* back safe and sound, and the mutineers
along with her, and you can set about it any way you choose.'

'You will give me full powers—to negotiate, for instance,
my lord?'

'I didn't mean that, damn it,' replied St Vincent. 'I meant
you could have any force you asked for. I could spare you
three ships of the line, if you want them. A couple of frigates.
Bomb-vessels.'

'It doesn't appear to be the kind of situation in which great
force would be of much use, my lord. Ships of the line would
seem to be superfluous.'

'I know that too, damn it.' The struggle in St Vincent's
mind was evident in his massive face. 'Those insolent rascals
can slip into the Seine's mouth in two shakes of a duck's
tail at the first sign of danger to themselves. It's brains that
are needed here, I know. That's why I sent for *you*, Hornblower.'

A nice compliment. Hornblower preened himself a little;

he was talking here on terms almost of equality to one of the greatest admirals who had ever hoisted his flag, and the sensation was extraordinarily pleasant. And the internal pressure which was mounting inside the First Lord suddenly forced out of him a yet more astonishing statement.

'And the men like you, Hornblower,' exploded St Vincent. 'Damn it, I don't know a man who doesn't. They'll follow you and listen to you. You're one of the officers the men talk about among themselves. They trust you and expect things of you—so do I, damn it, as you can see.'

'But if I talk to the men it will imply that I am negotiating with them, my lord.'

'No negotiations with mutineers!' blared St Vincent, striking the desk with a fist like a leg of mutton. 'We had enough of that in '94.'

'Then the *carte blanche* that you give me is no more than the usual naval officer's orders, my lord,' said Hornblower.

This was a serious matter; he was being sent out on an extremely difficult task, and would have to bear all the odium of failure should he be unsuccessful. He had never imagined himself bandying arguments with a First Lord, yet here he was actually doing so, impelled by sheer necessity. He studied St Vincent's expression again attentively; St Vincent was no fool and there was a thinking brain behind that craggy brow —he was fighting against his prejudices, preparing to dispense with them in the course of his duty.

'Very well then, Hornblower,' said the First Lord at length. 'I'll give you full powers. I'll have your orders drawn up to that effect. You will hold your appointment as Commodore, of course.'

'Thank you, my lord,' said Hornblower.

'Here's a list of the ship's company,' went on St Vincent. 'We have nothing here against any of them. Nathaniel Sweet, bos'n's mate—here's his signature—was first mate of a New-castle collier brig once—dismissed for drinking. Maybe he's the ringleader. But it may be any of 'em.'

St Vincent drew a sheaf of papers to himself and took up his pen—a handsome turkey-feather with one of the new-fangled gold nibs.

'What force do you require?'

'Something handy and small,' said Hornblower.

He had not the remotest idea how he was going to deal with this problem of recovering a vessel which had only to drop two miles to leeward to be irrecoverable, but his pride made him assume an appearance of self-confidence.

'There's *Porta Coeli,*' said St Vincent, raising his white eyebrows. 'Eighteen-gun brig—sister to *Flame,* in fact. She's at Spithead, ready to sail. Freeman's in command—he had the cutter *Clam* under your command in the Baltic. He brought you home, didn't he?'

'Yes, my lord.'

'Would she serve?'

'I think so, my lord.'

'Pellew's commanding the mid-Channel squadron. I'll send him orders to let you have any help you may request.'

'Thank you, my lord.'

'Wind's nor'westerly and steady,' said St Vincent, glancing up at the dial which repeated the indications of the weather-vane on the Admiralty roof. 'Glass is dropping, though. The sooner you're off the better. Where's your kit?'

'At Smallbridge, my lord. Almost on the road to Ports-mouth.'

'Good. Noon now. If you leave at three, you can be under way at midnight. I'll send Freeman his orders by post this minute. I wish you luck, Hornblower.'

'Thank you, my lord.'

Hornblower gathered his cloak round him, hitched up his sword, and took his leave. Before he had quitted the room a clerk had entered at the summons of St Vincent's jangling bell to take dictation of his order. Outside the north-westerly wind blew freshly, and he felt chilled and forlorn in his gay crimson and white silk.

In the Bay of the Seine

FREEMAN bent over the tallow that armed the bottom of the lead; a seaman held a lantern at his shoulder so as to let the light fall upon it. The master's mate and midshipman of the watch completed the group, a vignette of blackness and light in the massive darkness all around. Freeman was not hasty in reaching his decision; he peered at the sample brought up from the bottom of the sea first from one angle and then from another. He sniffed at it; he applied a forefinger to it and then carried the finger to his tongue.

'Sand and black shell,' he mused to himself.

128

Hornblower held back from the group; this was something Freeman could do better than he, although it would be nearly blasphemy to say so in public, seeing that he was a captain and Freeman a mere lieutenant.

'Maybe we're off Antifer,' said Freeman at length. He looked out of the light into the darkness towards where Hornblower was standing.

'Lay her on the other tack, if you please, Mr Freeman. And keep the lead going.'

Creeping about in the night off the treacherous Normandy coast was a nervous business, even though in the past twenty-four hours the wind had moderated to nothing more than a strong breeze. But Freeman knew what he was about; a dozen years spent in handling vessels in the soundings round the fringes of Europe had given him knowledge and insight obtainable in no other way. 'Maybe,' Freeman had said; but Hornblower could value that 'maybe' at its true worth. Freeman was confident about it. The *Porta Coeli* was off Cape Antifer, then, a trifle farther to leeward than he wished to be when dawn should come. He still had no plan in his head about how to deal with the *Flame* when he met her; there was no way round, as far as he could see, the simple geometrical difficulty that the mutineers, with Le Havre open to them on one side and Caen on the other, could not be cut off from taking refuge with the French if they wished to; for that matter, there were a dozen other inlets on the coast, all heavily protected by batteries, where the *Flame* could find a refuge. And any forcing of the matter might result easily enough in Chadwick being hoisted up to his yardarm, to dangle there as a dead man—the most horrible and dangerous incident in the history of the Navy since the murder of Pigott. But contact had to be made with the mutineers—that was clearly the first thing to do—and there was at least no harm in

trying to make that contact at a point as advantageous as
possible.

'Water's shoaling fast, sir,' said Freeman, suddenly—both
he and Hornblower had subconsciously been listening to the
cry of the leadsman in the chains. 'I should like to go about
again.'

'Certainly, Mr Freeman,' said Hornblower, formally.

They were creeping round Cape de la Hève, the northerly
point of the Seine estuary, just within which lies Le Havre.
There was a chance, a tiny one, that they might find themselves at dawn both to leeward of the *Flame* and between her
and France so that she would have no means of escape at all.
And the night was wearing on; it would not be long now
before daylight.

'You have a good man at the masthead, Mr Freeman?'

'Yes, Sir Horatio.'

He would have to tell the hands about the mission on
which they had been sent, even though that meant violating
the secrecy surrounding the mutiny. To ask them to fight
against a sister-ship, to fire into a British vessel, which might,
for all he knew, still be wearing her commissioning pendant
and her White Ensign, might cause hesitation if he called
upon them to do so without some preliminary warning. It
was almost daylight.

'Would you be so good as to turn up the hands, Mr
Freeman? I wish to address them.'

'Aye aye, sir.'

The pipes wailed through the brig, and the watch below
came streaming up through the hatchway, pouring sleepily
aft. Hornblower looked round for some point of vantage from
which he could address them; in a flush-decked vessel like
the *Porta Coeli* he had not the advantage of speaking down
into a waist from a quarter-deck. He swung himself up on to

the weather bulwark, balancing himself with a hand on the main backstay.

'Men,' he said, 'are you wondering what has sent you out here?'

Maybe they were, but the rather sleepy, apathetic, breakfastless lines before him showed little sign of it.

'Are you wondering what has sent me out to sea with you?'

By God, they *were* wondering that. There must have been speculation on the lower deck as to why a full commodore—and not only a commodore, but Hornblower of the legendary past—should have been sent to sea in a mere eighteen-gun brig.

'There is villainy afloat,' said Hornblower. 'British seamen have disgraced themselves. They have mutinied in the very presence of the enemy.'

He had the men's interest now, without a doubt. He had said the word 'mutiny' to these slaves of the lash and the whistle. Mutiny, the remedy for all their ills, which would give them freedom from the hardship of their lives, the cruelty and the danger, the foul food and the severance from all the amenities of life. Hornblower let a note of contempt creep into his voice.

'The crew of the *Flame,* our own sister-ship, has done this thing. Now they are sheltering here in this very bay of the Seine. Every man's hand is against them. The French have no use for mutineers, and it is our mission to dig these rats from their holes. They have betrayed England, forgotten their duty to King and Country. I expect most of them are honest but stupid, led astray by a few designing villains. It is those villains who must pay the price of their villainy, and we must see they have no chance of escape. If they are mad enough to offer fight, then we must fight them. If they surrender without bloodshed, that fact will be remembered in their favour when they are brought to trial. I want no bloodshed if I can help it—you know as well as I do that a cannon-shot will kill a man without stopping to ask whether he is a villain or just a fool. But if they want bloodshed, then we shall let them have it.'

Hornblower ended his speech, and looked over to Freeman to dismiss the men. It was a cheerless business making a speech to hungry men in a grey dawn, but Hornblower, darting glances at the men as they went about their business, saw that there was nothing to fear from the ship's company. They were buzzing with talk, of course, but news of mutiny would set any crew a-buzz, just as a village would be set a-buzz by news of a local murder. He had presented the case to them in such a way as to make it obvious to them that he expected them to obey his orders for dealing with the mutineers, and he had let no hint creep into his speech of his fear that they should be tempted to follow their example. That had not occurred to them yet—but it might, if they were allowed to ruminate over it. He must see that they were kept busy; the ordinary ship's routine was attending to that at the moment, for they were at work on the opening business of every naval day, washing down the decks before being piped to breakfast.

'Land!' yelled a voice from the masthead. 'Land on the port bow.'

It was rather thick weather, typical Channel weather for the end of the year, but in the growing light Hornblower could see the dark line against the grey. The growing light revealed the *Porta Coeli's* position, over towards the southern shore of the estuary of the Seine.

'That was an excellent piece of navigation last night, Mr Freeman.'

'Thank you, Sir Horatio.'

Hornblower would have added more words of warmer praise, if it had not been for Freeman's rather chilling manner; he supposed Freeman was entitled to be short-tempered before breakfast if he wished.

The leadsman's cry in the chains indicated that the water was shoaling again; they had left the middle ground far behind them and had now crossed the southerly channel of the estuary. There was still plenty of water for the *Porta Coeli;* she had been expressly designed for this very purpose of penetrating into inlets and estuaries, carrying the war as close to Bonaparte's shores as might be. Bonaparte's dominion stopped short at the line which the shot from his shore batteries could reach, and beyond that line England ruled supreme and unchallenged.

'Sail on the lee bow!' yelled the lookout.

Freeman swung himself up to the lee main-shrouds with the agility of an ape; braced against the ratlines, he trained his glass forward.

'A brig, sir,' he hailed down to Hornblower, and a few seconds later, 'That's *Flame* all right, sir.'

'Put the helm up and we'll bear down on her, Mr Freeman, if you please.'

Flame was exactly where one would expect to find her, close up under the lee of the land, sheltered from any gale from north-west round to east; and free to consult her own safety whether attacked by British or French. Soon Hornblower's own glass picked her out from the grey murk. A trim, beautiful little vessel, lying hove-to on the edge of the shoals. She showed no signs, at that distance at least, of any disorder on board. Hornblower wondered how many tele-scopes there were being trained upon the *Porta Coeli*, what anxious debate was being held on board by men recognizing the new arrival as the first move on the part of their Lordships of the Admiralty in reply to their suicidal ultimatum. Those men had ropes round their necks.

'She's waiting for us to come down to her,' said Freeman.

'I wonder for how long,' answered Hornblower.

A thin beam of watery sunshine broke through the greyness and lit up the *Flame* as she lay in the circle of Hornblower's glass. He suddenly saw her yards swing round; she put herself before the wind and began to move in the direction of Honfleur. Her foretopsail was conspicuously patched—a light cross against the darker material, as if she were some Crusading ship.

'They won't stand and wait for us,' said Freeman.

'Sail ho!' yelled the lookout again. 'Sail on the lee quarter!'

Telescopes swung round as if all were actuated by a single machine. A big ship with all plain sail set to the royals had appeared out of the mist beyond the middle ground, on a course rapidly diverging from that of the *Porta Coeli*. Hornblower recognized her instantly for what she was, and did not need Freeman's identification.

'French West-Indiaman,' said Freeman. 'With a clear run to Harbour-Grace.'

One of the rare ships to run the continental blockade, bearing an invaluable cargo of grain and sugar to ease Bonaparte's distress; she had taken advantage of the recent gale, which had blown the blockading squadrons from their stations, to dash up the Channel. A cargo delivered into the Seine, where centred the Imperial power, and whence diverged the whole road and canal systems, was worth two brought into some isolated inlet on the Biscay coast. The small British vessels of war, like the *Porta Coeli* and the

Flame, had been constructed and stationed to prevent this very thing.

'There'll be no catching her before she reaches Harbour-Grace,' muttered Freeman.

'Let her go, Mr Freeman,' said Hornblower, loudly. 'Our duty's with *Flame* at present. There goes ten pounds a man prize-money.'

There were enough hands within earshot to hear that speech; they would repeat it to the rest of the crew. No one who thought of the lost prize-money would feel any better disposed towards the mutineers.

Hornblower turned his attention back to the *Flame;* she was standing steadily and without hesitation on a course which would take her into Honfleur. It would not be long before she was in French power, and it would be foolish to press matters to such an extreme, even though it was a bitter pill to swallow, to admit a check.

'Oh, heave-to, Mr Freeman, please. Let's see what she does then.'

The *Porta Coeli* came up into the wind in response to sail and helm, Hornblower training round his glass to keep *Flame* under observation. The moment the *Porta Coeli's* manœuvre became apparent, the *Flame* imitated it, coming up into the wind and lying motionless, the white cross conspicuous on her foretopsail.

'Try bearing down on them again, Mr Freeman.'

Flame turned away instantly towards France.

'A wink's as good as a nod, Mr Freeman. Heave-to again.'

Clearly the mutineers had no intention of allowing the *Porta Coeli* to come any nearer than she was at present, well beyond cannon-shot. She would hand herself over to the French sooner than permit any closer approach.

'Mr Freeman, will you be so good as to have a boat hoisted out for me? I'll go and parley with the villains.'

That would be a sign of weakness, but the mutineers could be in no doubt about the weakness of his position and the corresponding strength of their own. It would be telling them nothing they did not know already, that they held Hornblower and the Lords of the Admiralty and the British Empire itself in a cleft stick. Freeman showed no signs of his doubts regarding the advisability of a valuable captain putting himself in the power of mutineers. Hornblower went below to pocket his orders; it might even be necessary to show the mutineers the full powers with which he had been entrusted—but it would be only in the last resort that he would do so; that would be letting the mutineers too much into their Lordships' confidence. The boat was overside with Brown at the tiller when Hornblower came on deck again; Hornblower went down the side and settled himself into the sternsheets.

'Give way!' ordered Brown; the oars bit the water and the boat began to crawl towards the *Flame*, dancing over the little waves of the estuary.

Hornblower watched the brig as they approached; she lay hove-to, but Hornblower could see that her guns were run out and her boarding-nettings rigged, and she had clearly no intention of being taken by surprise. The hands were at their guns, there were lookouts aloft, a warrant officer aft with a telescope under his arm—not a sign in the world of mutiny on board.

'Boat ahoy!' came the hail across the water.

Brown held up his four fingers, the universal signal that there was a captain in the boat—four fingers for the four side-boys demanded by ceremonial.

'Who are ye?' hailed the voice.

Brown looked round at Hornblower, received a nod from him, and hailed back.

'Commodore Sir Horatio Hornblower, K.B.'

'We'll allow Commodore Hornblower on board, but no one else. Come alongside, and we've cold shot here to drop into you if you play any tricks.'

Hornblower reached for the main-chains and swung himself up into them; a seaman raised the boarding-nettings so that he could struggle under them to the deck.

'Kindly tell your boat to sheer off, Commodore. We're taking no risks,' said a voice.

It was a white-haired old man who addressed him, the telescope under his arm marking him out as officer of the watch. White hair fluttered about his ears; sharp blue eyes in a wrinkled face looked at Hornblower from under white brows. The only thing in the least bizarre about his appearance was a pistol stuck in his belt. Hornblower turned and gave the required order.

'And now may I ask your business here, Commodore?' asked the old man.

'I wish to speak to the leader of the mutineers.'

'I an. captain of this ship. You can address yourself to me, Nathaniel Sweet, sir.'

'I have addressed myself to you as far as I desire, unless you are also the leader of the mutineers.'

'Then if you have done so, you can call back your boat and leave us, sir.'

An impasse already. Hornblower kept his eyes on the blue ones of the old man. There were several other men within earshot, but he could sense no wavering or doubt among them; they were prepared to support their captain. Yet it might be worth while speaking to them.

'Men!' said Hornblower, raising his voice.

'Belay that!' rapped out the old man. He whipped the pistol out of his belt and pointed it at Hornblower's stomach. 'One more word out of turn and you'll get an ounce of lead through you.'

Hornblower looked steadily back at him and his weapon; he was curiously unafraid, feeling as if he were watching move and counter-move in some chess game, without remembering that he himself was one of the pawns in it with his life at stake.

'Kill me,' he said with a grim smile, 'and England won't rest until you're swinging on a gallows.'

'England has sent you here to swing me on a gallows as it is,' said Sweet, bleakly.

'No,' said Hornblower. 'I am here to recall you to your duty to King and Country.'

'Letting bygones be bygones?'

'You will have to stand a fair trial, you and your confederates.'

'That means the gallows, as I said,' replied Sweet. 'The gallows for me, and I should be fortunate compared with some of these others.'

'A fair and honest trial,' said Hornblower, 'with every mitigating circumstance taken into consideration.'

'The only trial I would attend,' replied the old man, 'would be to bear witness against Chadwick. Full pardon for us— a fair trial for Chadwick. Those are our terms, sir.'

'You are foolish,' said Hornblower. 'You are throwing away your last chance. Surrender now, with Mr Chadwick unbound and the ship in good order, and those circumstances will weigh heavily in your favour at your trial. Refuse, and what have you to look for? Death. That is all. Death. What can save you from our country's vengeance? Nothing.'

'Belay that!' rapped the old man. He whipped the pistol out
and pointed it at Hornblower's stomach

'Begging your pardon, Captain, but Boney can,' interposed the old man, dryly.

'You trust Bonaparte's word?' said Hornblower, rallying desperately before this unexpected counter-attack. 'He'd like to have this ship, no doubt. But you and your gang? Bonaparte won't encourage mutiny—his power rests too much on his own army. He'll hand you back for us to make an example of you.'

It was a wild shot in the dark, and it missed its bull's-eye by an unmeasurable distance. Sweet stuck his pistol back into his belt and produced three letters from his pocket, waving them tauntingly in front of Hornblower.

'Here's a letter from the Military Governor of Harbour-Grace,' he said. 'That only promises us welcome. And here's a letter from the Prefect of the Department of the Inferior Seine. That promises us provisions and water should we need them. And here's a letter from Paris, sent down to us by post. It promises us immunity from arrest, civil rights in France, and a pension for every man from the age of sixty. That is signed "Marie Louise, Empress, Queen, and Regent.' Boney won't go back on his wife's word, sir.'

'You've been in communication with the shore?' gasped Hornblower. It was quite impossible for him to make any pretence at composure.

'We have,' said the old man. 'And if *you* had the chance before you, Captain, of being flogged round the fleet, you would have done the same.'

It was hopeless to continue the present discussion. At least at the moment, the mutineers were unassailable. The only terms to which they would listen would be their own. There was no sign of doubt or dissension on board. But maybe if they were allowed more time to think about it, maybe if they had a few hours in which to consider the fact that Hornblower himself was on their trail, doubt might creep in. A party might form determined to save their necks by recapturing the ship; they might get at the liquor—Hornblower was completely puzzled by the fact that a mutinous British crew was not all roaring drunk—*something* might happen. But he must make a fighting retreat, not ignominiously crawl overside with his tail between his legs.

'So you are traitors as well as mutineers?' he blared. 'I might have expected it. I might have guessed what kind of curs you are. I won't foul my lungs by breathing the same air as you.'

He turned to the side and hailed for his boat.

'We're the kind of curs,' said the old man, 'who will let you go when we could clap you down below in the orlop with Chadwick. We could give you a taste of the cat, Commodore Sir Horatio Hornblower. How would you like *that,* sir? Remember, to-morrow, that the flesh is still on your ribs because *we* spared you. Good morning to you, Captain.'

There was sting and venom in those last words; they called up pictures in Hornblower's imagination that made his flesh creep. He did not feel in the least dignified as he wriggled under the boarding-netting.

The *Flame* still rode peacefully to the wind as the boat danced back over the waves. Hornblower gazed from the *Flame* to the *Porta Coeli*, the two sister-ships, identical in appearance save for the white cross-shaped patch on the *Flame's* foretopsail. It was ironical that not even a trained eye could see any difference in appearance between the brig that was loyal to the King and the brig that was in open rebellion against him. The thought increased his bitterness; he had failed, utterly and completely, in his first attempt to win over the mutineers.

The boat was now half-way between the two brigs; with those two vessels under his command he could wage a lively war against the Normandy coast; he felt in his bones that he could set the whole Seine estuary in an uproar. His bitterness surged up stronger still, and then abruptly checked itself. An idea had come to him, and with the idea all the well-known old symptoms, the dryness in his throat, the tingling in his legs, the accelerated heart-beat. He swept his glance back and forth between the two brigs, excitement welling up inside him; calculations of wind and tide and daylight already formulating themselves, unsummoned, in his mind.

'Pull harder you men,' he said to the boat's crew, and they obeyed him, but the gig could not possibly travel fast enough to satisfy him in his new mood.

Hornblower went up the brig's side with a clumsy impetuosity that he could not restrain. Freeman was waiting for him on the quarter-deck, and Hornblower's hand was still at his hat when he gave his first order.

'Will you pass the word for the sailmaker, Mr Freeman? And I shall want his mates, and every hand who can use a needle and palm.'

'Aye aye, sir.'

Orders were orders, even when they dealt with such extraneous matters as making sails while negotiating with a mutinous crew. Hornblower stared over at the *Flame*, still lying hove-to out of gunshot. The mutineers held a strong, an unassailable position, one which no frontal attack could break, and whose flanks were impregnable. It would be a very roundabout route that could turn such a position; maybe he had thought of one.

A stoop-shouldered seaman was awaiting his attention, Freeman at his side.

'Swenson, sailmaker's mate, sir.'

'Thank you, Mr Freeman. You see that patched foretops'l, Swenson? Look at it well through this glass.'

The Swedish sailmaker took the telescope in his gnarled hands and levelled it to his eye.

'Mr Freeman, I want *Porta Coeli* to have a foretops'l just like that, so that no eye can see any difference between the two. Can that be done?'

Freeman looked at Swenson.

'Aye aye, sir, I can do that,' said Swenson, glancing from Freeman to Hornblower and back again. 'There's a bolt o' white duck canvas, an' with the old foretops'l—I can do it, sir.'

'I want it finished and ready to bend by four bells in the afternoon watch. Start work on it now.'

A little group had formed behind Swenson, those members of the crew whom inquiry had ascertained to have sailmaking experience. No one could see clearly as yet what was in Hornblower's mind, but they knew that he intended some devilment. The knowledge was a better tonic to discipline and the happiness of the ship than any ordinary ship's routine.

'Now see here, Mr Freeman,' said Hornblower, moving towards the rail. 'What I propose is this—*Flame* and *Porta Coeli* are as like as two peas and they'll be liker yet as soon as we have that foretops'l set. The mutineers have been in communication with the shore; they told me so, and, what's more, Mr Freeman, the place they've had dealings with is Le Havre—Harbour-Grace, Mr Freeman. Boney and the governor have promised them money and immunity to bring the *Flame* in. We'll go in instead. There's that West-Indiaman we saw come in this morning.'

'We'll bring her out, sir!'

'Maybe we will. God knows what we'll find inside, but we'll go in ready for anything. Pick twenty men and an officer, men you can rely on. Give each one his orders about what he is to do if we have a chance to take a prize—heads'ls, tops'ls, wheel, cutting the cable. You know about all that as well as I do. It'll be just at dusk that we stand in, if the wind doesn't change, and I don't think it will. It'll be strange if in the dark we don't contrive something to annoy the Frogs.'

'By God, sir, an' they'll think it's the mutineers! They'll think the mutiny was just a sham! They'll——'

'I hope they will, Mr Freeman.'

A Change of Foretopsails

IT was late afternoon when the *Porta Coeli,* apparently unable to reach any decision, stood away from the *Flame* and crossed the broad estuary with the wind blowing briskly on her port beam. The thick weather still persisted; she was far enough both from *Flame* and from Le Havre for the details to be quite obscure when she took in her foretopsail and substituted for it the patched one which an enthusiastic gang of toilers had made ready on deck abaft the foremast. Hurried work with paintbrush and paint erased one name and substituted the other; Hornblower and Freeman wore their plain pea-jackets over their uniforms, concealing their rank. Freeman kept his glass trained on the harbour as they stood in.

'That's the Indiaman, sir. At anchor. And there's a lighter

beside her. O' course, they wouldn't unload her at the quay. Not here, sir. They'd put her cargo into lighters an' barges, and send 'em up the river, to Rouen and Paris. O' course they would. I ought to ha' thought o' that before.'

Hornblower had already thought of it. His glass was sweeping the defences of the town; the forts of Ste Adresse and Tourneville on the steep cliff above the town; the twin lighthouses on Cape de la Hève—which for a dozen years had not shown a light—the batteries on the low ground beside the old jetty. These last would be the great danger to the enterprise; he hoped that the big forts above would not know of what was going on down below in time to open fire.

Hornblower turned to look at the western sky. Night was fast falling, and the thick weather on the horizon showed no signs of clearing. He wanted light enough to find his way, and darkness enough to cover him on his way out.

'Here's the pilot lugger standing out, sir,' said Freeman. 'They'll think we're *Flame* all right.'

'Very good, Mr Freeman. Set the men to cheering at the ship's side. Secure the pilot when he comes on board. I'll con her in.'

'Aye aye, sir.'

It was just the sort of order to suit the temperament of British seamen. They entered whole-heartedly into the spirit of the thing, yelling like lunatics along the bulwarks, waving their hats, dancing exuberantly, just as one would expect of a horde of mutineers. The *Porta Coeli* backed her maintop-sail, the lugger surged alongside, and the pilot swung himself into the mainchains.

'Lee braces!' roared Hornblower, the maintopsail caught the wind again, the wheel went over, and the *Porta Coeli* stood into the harbour, while Freeman put his shoulder between the pilot's shoulderblades and shot him neatly down the hatchway where two men were waiting to seize and pinion him.

'Pilot secured, sir,' he reported.

He, too, was obviously carried away by the excitement of the moment, infected even by the din the hands were making; his pose of amused irony had completely disappeared.

'Starboard a little,' said Hornblower to the helmsman. 'Meet her! Steady as you go!'

It would be the last word in ignominy if all their high hopes were to come to an end on the sandbanks guarding the entrance. Hornblower wondered if he would ever feel cool again.

'A cutter standing out to us, sir,' reported Freeman.

That might be a committee of welcome, or orders telling them where to berth—both at once, probably.

'Set the hands to cheering again,' ordered Hornblower. 'Have the boarding-party secured as they come on board.'

'Aye aye, sir.'

They were nearing the big Indiaman; she lay, her sails loose, swinging to a single anchor. There was a lighter beside her, but obviously little enough had been done so far towards unloading her. In the fading light Hornblower could just make out a dozen of her seamen standing at the ship's side gazing curiously at them. Hornblower backed the maintopsail again, and the cutter came alongside, and half a dozen officials climbed on to the *Porta Coeli's* deck. Their uniforms proclaimed their connection with the navy, the army, and the customs service, and they advanced slowly towards Hornblower, looking curiously about them as they did so. Hornblower was giving the orders that got the *Porta Coeli* under way again, and as she drew away from the cutter in the gathering darkness he wore her round and headed her for the Indiaman. Cutlasses suddenly gleamed about the new arrivals.

'Make a sound and you're dead men,' said Freeman.

Somebody made a sound, beginning to protest volubly. A seaman brought a pistol butt down on his head and the protests ended abruptly as the protester clattered on the deck. The others were hustled down the hatchway, too dazed and startled to speak.

'Very well, Mr Freeman,' said Hornblower, drawling the words so as to convey the impression that he felt perfectly at home here in the middle of a hostile harbour. 'You may hoist out the boats. Maintops'l aback!'

The shore authorities would be watching the brig's movements by what little light was left. If the *Porta Coeli* did anything unexpected, they would wonder idly what unknown condition on board had caused the harbourmaster's representative—now gagged and bound under hatches—to change his plans. The *Porta Coeli's* motion died away; the sheaves squealed as the boats dropped into the water, and the picked crews tumbled down into them. Hornblower leaned over the side.

'Remember men, don't fire a shot!'

The oars splashed as the boats pulled over to the Indiaman. It was practically dark by now; Hornblower could hardly follow the boats to the Indiaman's side fifty yards away, and he could see nothing of the men as they swarmed up her side. Faintly he heard some startled exclamations, and then one loud cry; that might puzzle the people on shore, but would not put them on their guard. Here were the boats returning, each pulled by the two men detailed for the work. The tackles were hooked on and the boats swayed up; as the sheaves squealed again Hornblower heard a crunching sound from the Indiaman, and a dull thump or two—the hand detailed to cut the cable was doing his work, and had actually remembered to carry the axe with him when he went up the ship's side. Hornblower felt the satisfaction of a job well done; his careful instruction of the boarding-party in the afternoon, his methodical allocation of duties to each individual man, and his reiteration of his orders until everyone thoroughly understood the part he had to play were bearing fruit.

Against the misty sky he saw the Indiaman's topsails changing shape; the men allotted to the task were sheeting them home. Thank God for a few prime seamen who, arriving in darkness in a strange ship, could find their way to the right places and lay their hands on the right lines without confusion. Hornblower saw the Indiaman's yards come round; in the darkness he could just see a black blur detach itself from her side, the lighter, cut adrift and floating away.

'You can square away, Mr Freeman, if you please,' he said. 'The Indiaman will follow us out.'

The *Porta Coeli* gathered way and headed for the southeastern exit of the harbour, the Indiaman close at her stern. For several long seconds there was no sign of any interest being taken in these movements. Then came a hail, apparently from the cutter which had brought the officials board. It was so long since Hornblower had heard or spoken French that he could not understand the words used.

'*Comment?*' he yelled back through the speaking-trumpet.

An irascible voice asked him again what in the name of the devil he thought he was doing.

'Anchorage—mumble—current—mumble—tide,' yelled Hornblower in reply.

This time the unknown in the cutter invoked the name of God instead of that of the devil.

'Who in God's name is that?'

'Mumble mumble mumble,' bellowed Hornblower back

again, and quietly to the helmsman, 'Bring her slowly round to port.'

Carrying on a conversation with the French authorities while taking a vessel down an involved channel—however well he had memorized the latter on the chart—taxed his resources.

'Heave-to!' yelled the voice.

'Pardon, Captain,' yelled Hornblower back. 'Mumble—anchor-cable—mumble—impossible.'

Another loud hail from the cutter, full of menace.

'Steady as you go,' cried Hornblower to the helmsman. 'Mr Freeman, a hand at the lead, if you please.'

He knew there was no chance of gaining any more precious seconds; by the time the leadsman was calling the depths and revealing the brig's design of evasion the shore authorities would be fully alert. A pinpoint of light stabbed the thin mist and the sound of a musket-shot came over the water; the cutter was taking the quickest method of attracting the attention of the shore batteries.

'Stand by to go about!' rasped Hornblower; this was the most ticklish moment of the outward passage.

The brig's canvas volleyed as she came round, and simultaneously there was a bigger tongue of red flame in the darkness and the sound of the cutter's six-pounder bow chaser, cleared away and loaded at last. Hornblower heard no sound of the ball. He was busy looking back at the Indiaman, dimly showing in the minute light of the brig's wake. She was coming about neatly. That master's mate—Calverly —whom Freeman had recommended for the command of the boarding-party was a capable officer, and must be highly praised when the time should come to send in a report.

And then from the jetty came a succession of flashes and a rolling roar; the big thirty-two pounders there had opened

fire at last. The sound of the last shot was instantly followed
by the noise of a ball passing close by; Hornblower had time
somehow to note how much he hated that noise. It would be
some minutes before he could tack again and stand directly
away from the jetty. It was a long time, on the other hand,
before the battery fired again. Here it came, the flash and the
roar, but this time there was no sound of any shot passing—
maybe the gunners had lost all sense of direction and elevation, which was easy enough in the darkness. And the flashes
from the guns were convenient in enabling Hornblower to
check his position. The Indiaman was still holding her course
in the brig's wake.

'By the mark eight!' called the leadsman.

He could lay her on the other tack now, and as he gave
the order the battery at the jetty again roared harmlessly.
They would be out of range by the time the gunners could
reload.

'A very good piece of work, Mr Freeman,' said Hornblower, loudly. 'All hands did their duty admirably.'

It would be a long time before the mutineers could clear
up their misunderstanding with the French authorities—
Hornblower could imagine the messengers hurrying at this
moment to warn the coastal defences at Honfleur and Caen—
even if eventually they should succeed in doing so. He had
turned the mutineers' position, cut off their retreat. He had
bearded Bonaparte under the batteries of his own capital
river. And there was the prize he had taken; at least a
thousand pounds, his share would be, when the prize-money
came to be reckoned up, and a thousand pounds was a
welcome sum of money, a gratifying sum.

A Three-Cornered Contest

'**M**R FREEMAN'S respects, sir,' said Brown, 'an' he said to tell you that day's just breaking, fairly clear, sir. Wind's backed to sou'-by-west, sir, during the night, blowin' moderate. We're hove-to, us an' the prize, an' it's the last of the floodtide now, sir.'

'Very good,' said Hornblower, rolling out of his cot. He was still heavy with sleep, and the tiny cabin seemed stuffy, as well as chilly, although the stern window was open.

'I'll have my bath,' said Hornblower, reaching a sudden decision. 'Go and get the wash-deck pump rigged.'

He felt unclean; although this was November in the Channel he could not live through another day without a bath. His ear caught some surprised and jocular comments from the hands rigging the pump as he came up through the hatchway, but he paid them no attention. He threw off his dressing-gown, and a puzzled and nervous seaman, in the half-light, turned the jet of the canvas hose upon him while another worked the pump. The bitterly cold sea-water stung as it hit his naked skin, and he leaped and danced and turned about grotesquely, gasping. The seaman did not realize it when he wanted the jet stopped, and when he tried to escape from it they followed him up across the deck.

'Avast there!' he yelled in desperation, half frozen and half drowned, and the merciless stream stopped.

Brown threw the big towel round him, and he scrubbed

his tingling skin, while he jumped and shivered with the stimulus of the cold.

'I'd be frozen for a week if I tried that, sir,' said Freeman, who had been an interested spectator.

'Yes,' said Hornblower, discouraging conversation.

His skin glowed delightfully as he put on his clothes in his cabin with the window shut, and his shivering ceased. He drank thirstily of the steaming coffee which Brown brought him, revelling in the pleasant and unexpected feeling of well-being that filled him. He ran lightheartedly on deck again. The morning was already brighter; the captured Indiaman could now be made out hove-to half a gunshot to leeward.

'Orders, Sir Horatio?' said Freeman, touching his hat.

Hornblower swept his glance round, playing for time. He had been culpably negligent of business; he had given no thought to his duty since he woke—since he went below to sleep, for that matter. He should order the prize back to England at once, but he could not do that without taking the opportunity of sending a written report back with her, and at this moment he simply hated the thought of labouring over a report.

'The prisoners, sir,' prompted Freeman.

Oh God, he had forgotten the prisoners. They would have to be interrogated and note made of what they had to say. Hornblower felt bone-lazy as well as full of well-being—an odd combination.

'They might have plenty to say, sir,' went on Freeman, remorselessly. 'The pilot talks some English, and we had him in the wardroom last night. He says Boney's been licked again. At a place called Leipzig, or some name like that. He says the Russians'll be over the Rhine in a week. Boney's back in Paris already. Maybe it's the end of the war.'

Hornblower and Freeman exchanged glances; it was a full

year since the world had begun to look for the end of the war, and many hopes had blossomed and wilted during that year. But the Russians on the Rhine! Even though the English army's entrance upon the soil of France in the south had not shaken down the Empire, this new invasion might bring that about.

'Sail-ho!' yelled the lookout, and in the same breath, 'She's the *Flame,* sir.'

There she was, as before; the parting mist revealed her for only a moment before closing round her again, and then a fresh breath of wind shredded the mist and left her in plain sight. Hornblower reached the decision he had so far been unable to make.

'Clear the ship for action, Mr Freeman, if you please. We're going to fetch her out.'

Of course, it was the only thing to do. During the night, within an hour of the cutting-out of the French Indiaman, the word would be sent flying round warning all French ports in the neighbourhood that the British brig with the white cross on her foretopsail was playing a double game, and only masquerading as a mutinous vessel. The news must have reached this side of the estuary by midnight. Any delay would give the mutineers a chance to reopen communication with the shore and to clear up the situation. Not an hour ought to be lost.

'See that the hands have some breakfast, if you please, Mr Freeman,' he said. 'And it would be best if the guns were not run out yet.'

'Aye aye, sir.'

It might be a long, hard battle, and the men should have their breakfast first. And running out the guns would tell the people in *Flame* that the *Porta Coeli* expected a fight. The more perfect the surprise, the greater the chance of an easy victory. Hornblower glowered at the *Flame* through his glass. He felt a dull, sullen rage against the mutineers who had caused all this trouble. The sympathy he had felt towards them when he was seated in the safety of the Admiralty was replaced now by a fierce resentment. The villains deserved hanging—the thought changed his mood so that he could smile as he met Freeman's eyes when the latter reported the brig cleared for action.

'Very good, Mr Freeman.'

His eyes were dancing with excitement; he looked over at *Flame* again just as a fresh hail came from the masthead.

'Deck, there! There's a whole lot of small craft putting out from the beach, sir. Headin' for *Flame* it looks like, sir.'

The mutineers' brig was going through the same performance as yesterday, heading towards the French coast just out of gunshot of the *Porta Coeli,* ready to take refuge sooner than fight; the mutineers must think the small craft a welcoming deputation, coming to escort them in. And there was thick weather liable to close in on them again at any moment. *Flame* was spilling the wind from her mainsail, her every action denoting increasing hesitation. Probably on her quarter-deck there was a heated argument going on, one party insisting on keeping out of range of the *Porta Coeli* while another hesitated before such an irrevocable action as going over to the French. Maybe there was another party clamouring to turn and fight—that was quite likely; and maybe even there was a party of the most timid or the least culpable who wished to surrender and trust to the mercy of a court martial. Certainly counsel would be divided. She was hauling on her sheet again now, on a straight course for Honfleur and the approaching gunboats; two miles of clear water separated her from the *Porta Coeli.*

'Those gunboats are closing in on her, sir,' said Freeman,

glass to eye. 'And that chasse-marée lugger's full of men. There's a gun.'

Someone in the *Flame* had fired a warning shot, perhaps to tell the French vessels to keep their distance until the debate on her deck had reached a conclusion. Then she wore round, as if suddenly realizing the hostile intent of the French, and as she wore the small craft closed in on her, like hounds upon a deer. Half a dozen shots were fired, too ragged to be called a broadside. The gunboats were heading straight at her, their sweeps out, six a side, giving them additional speed and handiness. Smoke spouted from their bows, and over the water came the deep-toned heavy boom of the twenty-four-pounders they mounted—a sound quite different from the higher-pitched, sharper bang of the *Flame's* carronades. The lugger ran alongside her, and through his glass Hornblower could see the boarders pouring on to the *Flame's* deck.

'I'll have the guns run out, Mr Freeman, if you please,' he said.

The situation was developing with bewildering rapidity—he had foreseen nothing like this. There was desperate fighting ahead, but at least it would be against Frenchmen and not against Englishmen. He could see puffs of smoke on the *Flame's* deck—some, at least, of the crew were offering resistance.

He walked forward a few yards, and addressed himself to the gunners.

'Listen to me, you men. Those gunboats must be sunk when we get in among 'em. One broadside for each will do that business for 'em if you make your shots tell. Aim true, at the base of their masts. Don't fire until you're sure you'll hit.'

'Aye aye, sir,' came a few voices in reply.

Hornblower found Brown beside him.

'Your pistols, sir. I loaded 'em afresh, an' primed 'em with new caps.'

'Thank you,' said Hornblower. He stuck the weapons into his belt, one on each side, where either hand could grasp them as necessary. It was like a boy playing at pirates, but his life might depend on those pistols in five minutes' time. He half drew his sword to see that it was free in its sheath, and he was already hastening back to take his stand by the wheel as he thrust it in again.

'Luff a little,' he said. 'Steady!'

Flame had flown up into the wind and lay all aback— apparently there was no one at the helm at the moment. The lugger was still alongside her, and the four gunboats, having taken in their sails, were resting on their oars, interposing between the *Porta Coeli* and the pair of ships. Hornblower could see the guns' crews bending over the twenty-four-pounders in their bows.

'Hands to the sheets, Mr Freeman, please. I'm going between them—there. Stand to your guns, men! Now, hard down!'

The wheel went over, and the *Porta Coeli* came about on the other tack, handily as anyone could desire. Hornblower heard the thunder of a shot close under her bows, and then the deck erupted in a flying shower of splinters from a jagged hole close to the mainmast bitts—a twenty-four-pound shot, fired upwards at close elevation, had pierced the brig's frail timbers, and continuing its flight, had burst through the deck.

'Ready about! Hard over!' yelled Hornblower, and the *Porta Coeli* tacked again into the narrow gap between two gunboats. Her carronades went off in rapid succession on both sides. Looking to starboard, Hornblower had one gunboat under his eye. He saw her there, half a dozen men

standing by the tiller aft, two men at each sweep amid-
ships tugging wildly to swing her round, a dozen men at the
gun forward. Then the shots came smashing in. The frail
frame of the gunboat—nothing more than a big rowing-boat
strengthened forward for a gun—disintegrated; her side caved
in under the shots as though under the blows of some vast
hammer. The sea poured in even as Hornblower looked; the
shots, fired with extreme depression, must have gone on
through the gunboat's bottom after piercing her side. The
dead weight of the gun in her bows took charge as her
stability vanished, and her bows surged under while her
stern was still above water. Then the gun slid out, relieving
her of its weight, and the wreck righted itself for an instant
before capsizing. A few men swam among the wreckage.
Hornblower looked over to port; the other gunboat had been
as hard hit, lying at that moment just at the surface with
the remains of her crew swimming by her. Whoever had been
in command of those gunboats had been a reckless fool to
expose the frail vessels to the fire of a real vessel of war—
even one as tiny as the *Porta Coeli*—as long as the latter
was under proper command. Gunboats were only of use to
batter into submission ships helplessly aground or dismasted.

The chasse-marée and the *Flame*, still alongside each other,
were close ahead.

'Mr Freeman, load with canister, if you please. We'll run
alongside the Frenchman. One broadside, and we'll board
her in the smoke.'

There was still time for Freeman to make the arrangements
as the *Porta Coeli* surged up towards the Frenchman, whose
name—the *Bonne Celestine* of Honfleur—was now visible on
her stern.

'Lay us alongside,' said Hornblower to the helmsman.
There was confusion on the decks of the *Bonne Celestine*;

The Bonne Celestine's *guns bellowed deafeningly*

Hornblower could see men running to the guns on her disengaged port side.

'Quiet, you men!' bellowed Hornblower. 'Quiet!'

Silence fell on the brig; Hornblower had hardly to raise his voice to make himself heard on the tiny deck.

'See that every shot tells, you gunners,' said Hornblower. 'Boarders, are you ready to come with me?'

Another yell answered him. Thirty men were crouching by the bulwarks with pikes and cutlasses; the firing of the broadside and the dropping of the mainsail would set free thirty more, a small enough force unless the broadside should do great execution and the untrained landsmen in the *Bonne Celestine* should flinch. Hornblower stole a glance at the helmsman, a grey-bearded seaman, who was coolly gauging the distance between the two vessels while at the same time watching the mainsail as it shivered as the *Porta Coeli* came to the wind. A good seaman, that—Hornblower made a mental note to remember him for commendation. The helmsman whirled the wheel over.

'Down mains'l,' roared Freeman.

The *Bonne Celestine's* guns bellowed deafeningly, and Hornblower felt powder grains strike his face as the smoke eddied round him. He drew his sword as the *Porta Coeli's* carronades crashed out, and the two vessels came together with a squealing of timber. He sprang upon the bulwark in the smoke, sword in hand; at the same moment a figure beside him cleared the bulwark in a single motion and dropped upon the *Bonne Celestine's* deck—Brown, waving a cutlass. Hornblower leaped after him, but Brown stayed in front of him, striking to left and right at the shadowy figures looming in the smoke. Here there was a pile of dead and wounded men, caught in the blast of canister from one of the *Porta Coeli's* carronades. Hornblower stumbled over a limb, and recovered himself in time to see a bayonet on the end of a musket lunging at him. A violent twisting of his body evaded the thrust. There was a pistol in his left hand, and he fired with the muzzle almost against the Frenchman's breast. Now the wind had blown the cannon-smoke clear. Forward some of the boarders were fighting with a group of the enemy cornered in the bow—the clash of the blades came clearly to Hornblower's ears—but aft there was not a Frenchman to be seen. Gibbons, master's mate, was at the halliards running down the tricolour from the masthead. At the starboard side lay the *Flame,* and over her bulwarks were visible French infantry shakoes; Hornblower saw a man's head and shoulders appear, saw a musket being pointed. It shifted its aim from Gibbons to Hornblower, and in that instant Hornblower fired the other barrel of his pistol, and the Frenchman fell down below the bulwarks, just as a fresh wave of boarders came pouring on board from the *Porta Coeli.*

'Come on!' yelled Hornblower—it was desperately important to make sure of the *Flame* before a defence could be organized.

The brigs stood higher out of the water than did the chassemarée; this time they had to climb upward. He got his left elbow over the bulwark, and tried to swing himself up, but his sword hampered him.

'Help me, damn you!' he snarled over his shoulder, and a seaman put his shoulder under Hornblower's stern and heaved him up with such surprising goodwill that he shot over the bulwarks and fell on his face in the scuppers on the other side, his sword slithering over the deck. He started to crawl forward towards it, but a sixth sense warned him of danger, and he flung himself down and forward inside the sweep of a cutlass, and cannoned against the shins of the man who wielded it. Then a wave of men burst over him, and he was kicked and trodden on and then crushed beneath a writhing body with which he grappled with desperate strength. He could hear Brown's voice roaring over him, pistols banging, sword-blades clashing before sudden silence fell round him. The man with whom he was struggling went suddenly limp and inert, and then was dragged off him. He rose to his feet.

'Are you wounded, sir?' asked Brown.

'No,' he answered. Three or four dead men lay on the deck; aft a group of French soldiers with a French seaman or two among them stood by the wheel, disarmed, while two British sailors, pistol in hand, stood guard over them. A French officer, blood dripping from his right sleeve, and with tears on his cheeks—he was no more than a boy—was sitting on the deck, and Hornblower was about to address him when his attention was suddenly distracted.

'Sir! Sir!'

It was an English seaman he did not recognize, in a striped shirt of white and red, his pigtail shaking from side to side as he gesticulated with the violence of his emotion.

'Sir! I was fightin' against the Frogs. Your men saw me. Me an' these other lads here.'

He motioned behind him to an anxious little group of sea-men who had heretofore hung back, but now came forward, some of them bursting into speech, all of them nodding their heads in agreement.

'Mutineers?' asked Hornblower. In the heat of battle he had forgotten about the mutiny.

'I'm no mutineer, sir. I did what I had to or they'd 'a killed me. Ain't that so, mates?'

'Stand back, there!' blared Brown; there was blood on the blade of his cutlass.

A vivid prophetic picture suddenly leaped into Horn-blower's mind's eye—the court martial, the semi-circle of judges in glittering full dress, the tormented prisoners, tongue-tied, watching, only half understanding, the proceedings which would determine their lives or deaths, and he himself giving his evidence, trying conscientiously to remember every word spoken on both sides; one word remembered might make the difference between the lash and the rope.

'Arrest those men!' he snapped. 'Put them under confinement.'

'Sir! Sir!'

'None o' that!' growled Brown.

Remorseless hands dragged the protesting men away.

'Where are the other mutineers?' demanded Hornblower.

'Down below, sir, I fancies,' said Brown. 'Some o' the Frenchies is down there, too.'

Odd how a beaten crew so often scuttled below. Hornblower honestly believed that he would rather face the fighting madness of the victors on deck than surrender ignominiously in the dark confines of the 'tween-decks.

A loud hail from the *Porta Coeli* came to his ears.

'Sir Horatio!' hailed Freeman's voice. 'We'll be all aground if we don't get way on the ships soon. I request permission to cast off and make sail.'

'Wait!' replied Hornblower.

He looked round him; the three ships locked together, prisoners under guard here, there, and everywhere. Below decks, both in the *Bonne Celestine* and in the *Flame,* there were enemies still unsecured, probably many more in total than he had men under his orders. A shattering crash below him, followed by screams and cries; the *Flame* shook under a violent blow. Hornblower remembered the sound of a cannon-shot striking on his inattentive ears a second before; he looked round. The two surviving gunboats were resting on their oars a couple of cables' lengths away, their bows pointing at the group of ships. Hornblower could guess they were in shoal water, almost immune from attack. A jet of smoke from one of the gunboats, and another frightful crash below, and more screams. Those twenty-four-pounder balls were probably smashing through the whole frail length of the brig, whose timbers could resist their impact hardly better than paper. Hornblower plunged into the urgency of the business before him like a man into a raging torrent which he had to swim.

'Get those hatches battened down, Brown!' he ordered. 'Put a sentry over each. Mr Gibbons!'

'Sir?'

'Secure your hatches. Get ready to make sail.'

'Aye aye, sir.'

'What topmen are there here? Man the halliards. Who can take the wheel? Wheel none of you? Mr Gibbons! Have you a quartermaster to spare? Send one here immediately. Mr Freeman! You can cast off and make sail. Rendezvous at the other prize.'

Another shot from those accursed gunboats crashed into the *Flame's* stern below him. Thank God the wind was off shore and he could get clear of them. The *Porta Coeli* had set her boom-mainsail again and had got clear of the *Bonne Celestine;* Gibbons was supervising the setting of the latter's lug-mainsail while half a dozen hands boomed her off from the *Flame.*

'Hoist away!' ordered Hornblower as the vessels separated. 'Hard a-starboard, Quartermaster.'

A sound overside attracted his attention. Men—mutineers or Frenchmen—were scrambling out through the shot-holes and hurling themselves into the sea, swimming towards the gunboats. Hornblower saw the white hair of Nathaniel Sweet trailing on the surface of the water as he struck out, twenty feet away from him. Of all the mutineers he was the one who most certainly must not be allowed to escape. For the sake of England, for the sake of the service, he must die. The seaman acting as sentry at the after hatchway did not look as if he were a capable marksman.

'Give me your musket,' said Hornblower, snatching it.

He looked at priming and flint as he hurried back to the taffrail. He trained the weapon on the white head, and pulled the trigger. The smoke blew back into his face, obscuring his view only for a moment. The long white hair was visible for a second at the surface when he looked again, and then it sank, slowly, out of sight. Sweet was dead. Maybe there was an old widow who would bewail him, but it was better that Sweet was dead. Hornblower turned back to the business of navigating the *Flame* back to the rendezvous.

Lebrun makes a proposal

THIS fellow Lebrun was an infernal nuisance, demanding a private interview in this fashion. Hornblower had quite enough to do as it was; the gaping shot-holes in *Flame's* side had to be patched sufficiently well to enable her to recross the Channel; the exiguous crew of the *Porta Coeli*—not all of them seamen by any means—had to be distributed through no fewer than four vessels (the two brigs, the Indiaman, and the chasse-marée), while at the same time adequate guard must be maintained over more than a hundred prisoners of one nationality or another; the mutineers must be supervised so that nothing could happen to prejudice their trial; worst of all, there was a long report to be made out. Some people would think this last an easy task, seeing that there was a long string of successes to report, two prizes taken, the *Flame* recaptured, most of the mutineers in irons below decks and their ringleader slain by Hornblower's own hand. But there was the physical labour of writing it out, and Hornblower was very weary.

Hornblower shook himself free from a clinging tangle of thoughts to find himself still staring abstractedly at the young seaman who had brought to him Freeman's message regarding Lebrun's request.

'My compliments to Mr Freeman, and he can send this fellow in to me,' he said.

An armed guard brought Lebrun into the cabin, and Hornblower looked him keenly over. He was one of the half-dozen prisoners taken when the *Porta Coeli* came into Le Havre, one of the deputation which had mounted her deck to welcome her under the impression that she was the *Flame* coming in to surrender.

'Monsieur speaks French?' said Lebrun.

'A little.'

'More than a little, if all the tales about Captain Hornblower are true,' replied Lebrun.

'What is your business?' snapped Hornblower, cutting short this Continental floweriness. Lebrun was a youngish man, of olive complexion, with glistening white teeth, who conveyed a general impression of oiliness.

'I am *adjoint* to Baron Momas, Mayor of Le Havre.'

'Yes?' Hornblower tried to show no sign of interest, but he knew that under the Imperial régime the mayor of a large town like Le Havre was a most important person, and that his *adjoint*—his assistant, or deputy—was a very important permanent official.

'The firm of Momas Frères is one you must have heard of. It has traded with the Americas for generations—the history of its rise is identical with the history of the development of Le Havre itself.'

'Yes?'

'Similarly, the war and the blockade have had a most disastrous effect upon the fortunes both of the firm of Momas and upon the city of Le Havre.'

'Yes?'

'The *Caryatide,* the vessel that you so ingeniously captured two days ago, monsieur, might have restored the fortunes of us all—a single vessel running the blockade, as you will readily understand, is worth ten vessels arriving in peacetime.'

'Yes?'

'M. le Baron and the city of Le Havre will be desperate,

I have no doubt, as the result of her capture before her cargo could be taken out.'

'Yes?'

The two men eyed each other, like duellists during a pause, Hornblower determined to betray none of the curiosity and interest that he felt, and Lebrun hesitating before finally committing himself.

'I take it, monsieur, that anything further I have to say will be treated as entirely confidential.'

'I promise nothing. In fact, I can only say that it will be my duty to report anything you say to the Government of His Majesty of Great Britain.'

'They will be discreet for their own sake, I expect,' ruminated Lebrun.

'His Majesty's ministers can make their own decisions,' said Hornblower.

'You are aware, monsieur,' said Lebrun, obviously taking the plunge, 'that Bonaparte has been defeated in a great battle at Leipzig?'

'Yes.'

'The Russians are on the Rhine.'

'That is so.'

'The Russians are on the Rhine!' repeated Lebrun, marvelling. The whole world, pro-Bonaparte or anti-Bonaparte, was marvelling that the massive Empire should have receded half across Europe in those few short months.

'And Wellington is marching on Toulouse,' added Hornblower—there was no harm in reminding Lebrun of the British threat in the south.

'That is so. The Empire cannot much longer endure.'

'I am glad to hear your opinion in the matter.'

'And when the Empire falls there will be peace, and when peace comes trade will recommence.'

'Without a doubt,' said Hornblower, still a little mystified.

'Profits will be enormous during the first few months. All Europe has for years been deprived of foreign produce. At this moment genuine coffee commands a price of over a hundred francs a pound.'

Now Lebrun was showing his hand, more involuntarily than voluntarily. There was a look of avarice in his face which told Hornblower much.

'All this is obvious, monsieur,' said Hornblower, noncommittally.

'A firm which was prepared for the moment of peace, with its warehouses gorged with colonial produce ready to distribute, would greatly benefit. It would be far ahead of its competitors. There would be millions to be made. Millions.' Lebrun was obviously dreaming of the possibility of finding some of those millions in his own pocket.

'I have a great deal of business to attend to, monsieur,' said Hornblower. 'Have the goodness to come to the point.'

'His Majesty of Great Britain might well allow his friends to make those preparations in advance,' said Lebrun, the words coming slowly; well they might, for they could take him to the guillotine if Bonaparte ever heard of them. Lebrun was offering to betray the Empire in exchange for commercial advantages.

'His Majesty would first need undeniable proof that his friends *were* his friends,' said Hornblower. 'You may tell me the nature of your offer, but I can make no promises of any sort in return.'

'Supposing the city of Le Havre declared itself against the Empire, declared itself for Louis XVIII?'

The possibility had occurred to Hornblower, but he had put it aside as being potentially too good to be true.

'Supposing it did?' he said cautiously.

'It might be the example for which the Empire is waiting.
It might be infectious. Bonaparte could not survive such a
blow.'

'He has survived many blows.'

'But none of this sort. And if Le Havre declared for the
King the city would be in alliance with Great Britain. The
blockade could not continue to apply. Or if it did a licence
to import could be granted to the house of Momas Frères,
could it not?'

'Possibly. Remember, I make no promises.'

'And when Louis XVIII was restored to the throne of his
fathers he would look with kindness upon those who first
declared for him,' said Lebrun. 'The *adjoint* to Baron Momas
might expect to find a great career open to him.'

'No doubt of that,' agreed Hornblower. 'But—you have
spoken of your own sentiments. Can you be sure of those
of M. le Baron? And whatever may be M. le Baron's sentiments, how can he be sure that the city would follow him
should he declare himself?'

'I can answer for the Baron, I assure you, sir. I know—I
have certain knowledge of his thoughts.'

Probably Lebrun had been spying on his master on behalf
of the Imperial Government, and had no objection to apply-
ing his knowledge in another and more profitable cause.

'But the other authorities in the town? The military
governor? The Prefect of the Department?'

'Some of them would be safe. I know their sentiments as
well as I know Baron Momas'. The others—a dozen well-
timed arrests, carried out simultaneously, an appeal to the
troops in the barracks, the arrival of British forces (*your*
forces, sir), a heartening proclamation to the people, the
declaration of a state of siege, the closing of the gates, and
it would be all over. Le Havre is well fortified, as you know,

sir. Only an army and a battering train could retake it, and
Bonaparte has neither to spare. The news would spread like
wildfire through the Empire, however Bonaparte tried to
stop it.'

This man Lebrun had ideas and vision, whatever might be
thought of his morals. That was a neat thumbnail sketch
he had drawn of a typical *coup d'état*. If the attempt were
successful the results would be profound. Even if it were to
fail, loyalty throughout the Empire would be shaken. There
would be little enough to risk losing in supporting Lebrun's
notions, and the gains might be immense.

'Monsieur,' said Hornblower, 'so far I have been patient.
But in all this time you have made me no concrete proposal.
Words—nebulous ideas—hopes—wishes, that is all, and I am
a busy man, as I told you. Please be specific. And speedy,
if that is not too much trouble to you.'

'I shall be specific, then. Set me on shore—as an excuse I
could be sent to arrange a cartel for the exchange of prisoners.
Let me be able to assure M. le Baron of your instant support.
In the three days before next Monday I can complete the
arrangements. Meanwhile, you remain close in the vicinity
with all the force you can muster. The moment we secure
the citadel we shall send up the white flag, and the moment
you see that you enter the harbour and overawe any possible
dissentients. In return for this—a licence to Momas Frères
to import colonial produce, and your word of honour as
a gentleman that you will inform King Louis that it
was I, Hercule Lebrun, who first suggested the scheme to
you.'

'Ha—h'm,' said Hornblower. He had to have time to think.
The long conversation in the French which he was not
accustomed to using had been exhausting. He lifted his voice
in a bellow to the sentry outside the door.

'Pass the word for the armed guard to take this prisoner away.'

'Sir!' protested Lebrun.

'I will give you my decision in an hour,' said Hornblower. 'Meanwhile for appearance's sake you must be treated harshly.'

Bush arrives
with Reinforcements

THE tricolour was still flying over the citadel—the
fortress of Ste Adresse—of Le Havre; Hornblower
could see it through his glass as he stood on the deck
of the *Flame,* which was creeping along under easy sail, just
out of range of the shore batteries. He had decided, inevitably,
to assist Lebrun in his scheme. He was telling himself again,
at that very moment, and for the thousandth time, that there
was much to gain whatever the result, and little enough to
lose. Only Lebrun's life, and perhaps Hornblower's reputation. The Government could refuse to honour the promises

173

he had made regarding import licences; they could come out with a bold announcement that they had no intention of recognizing Louis XVIII's pretensions; they could rap him over the knuckles very sharply indeed for most of his actions since recapture of the *Flame*.

He had used his powers to pardon forty mutineers, all the seamen and boys, in fact. To keep the mutineers as well as the prisoners under guard, and to provide prize crews for the two prizes, would have called for the services of every man at his disposal. He would hardly have had enough to handle the vessels, and certainly he could have attempted nothing further. As it was, he had relieved himself of all these difficulties by a few simple decisions. Every Frenchman had been sent on shore in the *Bonne Celestine* under flag of truce, with Lebrun ostensibly to arrange for their exchange; the Indiaman had been manned by a minimum crew and sent with despatches to Pellew and the Mid-Channel Squadron, and he had been able to retain the two brigs, each at least sufficiently manned, under his own command. That had been a convenient way of getting rid of Chadwick, too—he had been entrusted with the despatches and the command of the Indiaman.

By now those despatches should have passed through Pellew's hands, and, their contents noted, might even be on their way to Whitehall. The wind had been fair for the Indiaman to have fetched the Mid-Channel Squadron off the Start—fair, too, for the reinforcements Hornblower had asked for to make their way to him. Pellew would send them, he knew.

Hornblower glanced out to seaward, where, dim on the horizon, the *Porta Coeli* patrolled in the mist. She would halt the reinforcements before they could be sighted from the shore, for there was no reason why the authorities in Le Havre should be given the least chance to think that anything unusual portended.

'Keep a sharp lookout for any signal from the *Porta Coeli*,' he said sharply to the midshipman of the watch.

'Aye aye, sir.'

It was late afternoon before the expected interruption came.

'Signal from *Porta Coeli*, sir! Eighteen—fifty-one—ten. That's friendly ships in sight, bearing nor'west.'

'Very good. Ask their numbers.'

This must be the reinforcements sent by Pellew. The signal hands bent on the flags and hauled away at the halliards; it was several minutes before the midshipman noted the reply and translated it by reference to the list.

'*Nonsuch*, 74, Captain Bush, sir.'

'Bush, by God!'

The exclamation leaped uncontrolled from Hornblower's lips; the difficulties that surrounded him were chased away as though by holy water at the thought of his old staunch matter-of-fact friend being only just over the horizon. Of course Pellew would send Bush if he were available, knowing the friendship that had so long existed between him and Hornblower.

'*Camilla*, 36, Captain Howard, sir.'

He knew nothing about Howard whatever. He looked at the list—a captain of less than two years' seniority. Presumably Pellew had selected him as junior to Bush.

'Very good. Reply—"Commodore to——" '

'*Porta's* still signalling, begging your pardon, sir. "*Nonsuch* to Commodore. Have—on board—three hundred—marines —above—complement." '

Good for Pellew. He had stripped his squadron to give Hornblower a landing force that could make itself felt.

Three hundred marines, and the *Nonsuch's* detachment as well, and a body of seamen. He could march five hundred men into Le Havre should the opportunity arise.

'Very good. Make "Commodore to *Nonsuch* and *Camilla*. Delighted to have you under my command." '

Hornblower looked again over at Le Havre. He looked up at the sky, he gauged the strength of the wind, remembered the state of the tide, calculated the approach of night. Over there Lebrun must be bringing his plans to fruition, to-night if at all. He must be ready to strike his blow.

'Make "Commodore to all vessels. Join me here after dark. Night signal two lanterns horizontally at fore yardarms." '

'—fore yardarms. Aye aye, sir,' echoed the midshipman, scribbling on his slate.

It was good to see Bush again, to shake his hand in welcome as he hoisted himself in the darkness on to the *Flame's* deck. It was good to sit in the stuffy little cabin with Bush and Howard and Freeman as he told them about his plans for the morrow.

They nodded, turning their eyes to the chart spread out in front of them.

'No questions?'

'No, sir.'

'I know this is only the sketchiest plan. There will be contingencies, emergencies. No one can possibly foresee what will happen. But of one thing I am certain, and that is that the ships of this squadron will be commanded in a way that will bring credit to the service. Captain Bush and Mr Freeman have acted with bravery and decision under my own eyes too often, and I know Captain Howard too well by reputation for me to have any doubt about that. When we attack Havre, gentlemen, we shall be turning a page, we shall be writing the end of a chapter in the history of tyranny.'

They were pleased with what he said, and they could have no doubt regarding his sincerity, because he spoke from his heart. They smiled as he met their eyes. This final speech of his had been uttered to get them into good humour—and yet he had meant every word of it. No, not quite—he was still almost ignorant of Howard's achievements. To that extent the speech was formal. But it had served its purpose.

'Then we have finished with business, gentlemen. What can I offer you by way of entertainment? Captain Bush can remember games of whist played on the nights before going into action. But he is by no means an enthusiastic whist player.'

That was understating the case—Bush was the most reluctant whist player in the world and he grinned sheepishly in acknowledgment of Hornblower's gentle gibe.

'You should have a night's rest, sir,' he said, speaking, as the senior, for the other two, who looked to him for guidance.

'I should get back to my ship, sir,' echoed Howard.

'So should I, sir,' said Freeman.

Hornblower was genuinely sorry to see them go. He stood on the deck of the *Flame* and watched their gigs creep away in the black winter night, while the pipe of the bos'n's mate was calling the hands for the middle watch. It was piercing cold, especially after the warm stuffiness of the cabin, and he felt suddenly even more lonely than usual, maybe as a result. Here in the *Flame* he had only two watch-keeping officers, borrowed from the *Porta Coeli;* to-morrow he would borrow another from the *Nonsuch* or the *Camilla*. To-morrow? That was to-day. And to-day perhaps Lebrun's attempt to gain control of Le Havre might be successful. To-day he might be dead.

Le Havre declares for King Louis

IT was as misty as might be expected of that season and place when day broke, or rather when the grey light crept almost unnoticed into one's consciousness. The *Porta Coeli* was dimly visible, an almost unnoticeable denser nucleus in the fog. Hailing her at the top of his lungs, Hornblower received the faint reply that *Nonsuch* was in sight astern of her, and a few seconds later the additional information that *Camilla* was in sight of *Nonsuch*. He had his squadron in hand, then, and there was nothing to do but wait, and to ponder for the hundredth time over the question as to how the hands, barefooted with the icy water surging round their feet, could possibly bear their morning duty of washing down the decks. But they were laughing and skylarking as they did it; the British seaman was of tough material. Presumably the lower deck guessed that there was something in the wind, that this concentration of force portended fresh action, and they found the prospect exhilarating.

He himself was in a fever of anxiety, turning over in his mind the arrangements he had finally made with Lebrun before sending him ashore. They were simple enough; absurdly simple, it seemed to him now. The whole plan seemed a feeble thing with which to overturn an Empire that dominated Europe. Yet a conspiracy should be simple—the more elaborate the machinery the greater the chance of its breaking down. That was one reason why he had insisted on daylight for his part of the business. He had dreaded the possible mishaps if he had plunged ashore in darkness into an unknown town with his little army. Daylight doubled the chances of success while it doubled at least the possible loss in case of failure.

Hornblower looked at his watch—for the last ten minutes he had been fighting down the urge to look at it.

'Mr Crawley,' he said, to the master's mate who was his new first lieutenant in the *Flame*. 'Beat to quarters and clear the brig for action.'

The wind was a light air from the east, as he had expected. Fetching into Le Havre would be a ticklish business, and he was glad that he had resolved to lead in the small and hardy *Flame* so as to show the way to the ponderous old *Nonsuch*.

'Ship cleared for action, sir,' reported Crawley.

'Very good.'

Hornblower looked at his watch—it was fully a quarter-hour yet before he should move in.

'Remember, Mr Crawley,' he said, 'if I am killed as we go in, the *Flame* is to be laid alongside the quay. Captain Bush is to be informed as soon as possible, but the *Flame* is to go on.'

'Aye aye, sir,' said Crawley. 'I'll remember.'

Damn his eyes, he need not be so infernally ordinary about it. From the tone of Crawley's voice one might almost assume that he expected Hornblower to be killed. Hornblower turned away from him and walked the deck briskly to shake off the penetrating cold. He looked along at the men at their stations.

'Skylark, you men,' he ordered. 'Let's see how you can jump.'

There was no use going into action with men chilled to numbness. The men at the guns and waiting at the sheets began to caper at their posts.

'Jump, you men, jump!'

Hornblower leaped grotesquely up and down to set them an example; he wanted them thoroughly warmed up. He flapped his arms against his sides as he leaped, the epaulettes of the full-dress uniform he was wearing pounded on his shoulders.

'Higher than that! Higher!'

His legs were beginning to ache, and his breath came with difficulty, but he would not stop before the men did, although he soon came to regret the impulse which had made him start.

'Still!' he shouted at last, the monosyllable taking almost the last breath from his body. He stood panting, the men grinning.

'Horny for ever!' yelled an unidentifiable voice forward, and a ragged cheer came from the men.

'Silence!'

Brown was beside him with his pistols, a twinkle in his eye.

'Take that grin off your face!' snapped Hornblower.

There would be another Hornblower legend growing up in the Navy, similar to the one about the hornpipe danced on the deck of the *Lydia* during the pursuit of the *Natividad*. Hornblower pulled out his watch, and when he had replaced it took up his speaking-trumpet.

'Mr Freeman! I am going about on the other tack. Hail the squadron to tack in succession. Mr Crawley!'

'Sir!'

'Two hands at the lead, if you please.'

One man might be killed, and Hornblower wanted no possible cessation in the calling of soundings.

'Headsail sheets! Mains'l sheets!'

The *Flame* went about on the starboard tack, making

about three knots under fore and aft sail in the light breeze.
Hornblower saw the shadowy *Porta Coeli* follow the *Flame's*
example. Behind her, and invisible, was the old *Nonsuch*—
Hornblower had still to set eyes on her since her arrival.
He had not seen her, for that matter, since he quitted her to
catch the typhus in Riga. Good old Bush. It gave Hornblower some comfort to think that he would be supported
to-day by the *Nonsuch's* thundering broadsides and Bush's
stolid loyalty.

The leadsmen were already chanting the depths as the
Flame felt her way up the fairway towards Le Havre. Hornblower wondered what was going on in the city, and then
petulantly told himself that he would know soon enough.
It seemed to him as if he could remember every single word
of the long discussion he had had with Lebrun, when between
them they had settled the details of Lebrun's harebrained
scheme. They had taken into account the possibility of fog
—any seaman would be a fool who did not do so in the Bay
of the Seine in winter.

'*Qui va là?*' screamed a voice through the fog from close
overside; Hornblower could just see the French boat which
habitually rowed guard over the entrance in thick weather.
The guard-boat, as Hornblower and Lebrun had agreed,
would not be easily diverted from its duty.

'Despatches for M. le Baron Momas,' hailed Hornblower
in return.

The confident voice, the fluent French, the use of Momas'
name, might all gain time for the squadron to enter.

'What ship?'

It was inconceivable that the seamen in the guard-boat
did not recognize the *Flame*—the question must be a merely
rhetorical one asked while the puzzled officer in command
collected his thoughts.

'British brig *Flame*,' called Hornblower; he had the helm put over at that moment to make the turn past the point.

'Heave-to, or I will fire into you!'

'If you fire, you will have the responsibility,' replied Hornblower. 'We bear despatches for Baron Momas.'

It was a fair wind now for the quay. The turn had brought the guard-boat close alongside; Hornblower could see the officer standing up in the bows beside the bow-gun, a seaman at his shoulder with a glowing linstock in his hand. Hornblower's own full-dress uniform must be visible and cause some delay, too, for men expecting to fight would not be expected to wear full dress. He saw the officer give a violent start, having caught sight of the *Porta Coeli* looming up in the mist astern of the *Flame*. He saw the order given, saw the spark thrust on the touch-hole. The three-pounder roared, and the shot crashed into the *Flame's* side. That would give the alarm to the batteries at the point and above the quay.

'We do not fire back,' he hailed—maybe he could gain a little more time, and maybe that time would be of use, although he doubted it.

Here inside the harbour the mist was not so thick. He could see the shadowy shape of the quay rapidly defining itself. In the next few seconds he would know if this were a trap or not, if the batteries should open in a tempest of flame. One part of his mind raced through the data, while another part was working out how to approach the quay. He could not believe that Lebrun was playing a double game, but if it were so only he and the *Flame* would be lost—the other vessels would have a chance to get clear.

'Luff!' he said to the helmsman. There were a few busy seconds as he applied himself to the business of bringing the *Flame* alongside the quay as speedily as possible and yet without damaging her too severely. She came alongside with a creak and a clatter, the fenders groaning as if in agony. Hornblower sprang on to the bulwark and from there to the quay, sword, cocked hat, epaulettes and all. He could not spare time to look around, but he had no doubt that the *Porta Coeli* had anchored, ready to give assistance where necessary, and that the *Nonsuch* in her turn was nearing the quay, her marines drawn up ready for instant landing. He strode up the quay, his heart pounding. There was the first battery, the guns glaring through the embrasures. He could see movement behind the guns, and more men running to the battery from the guardhouse in the rear. Now he had reached the edge of the moat, his left hand held up in a gesture to restrain the men at the guns.

'Where is your officer?' he shouted.

There was a momentary delay, and then a young man in blue and red artillery uniform sprang upon the parapet.

'What do you want?' he asked.

'Tell your men not to fire,' said Hornblower. 'Have you not received your new orders?'

The full dress, the confident bearing, the extraordinary circumstances puzzled the young artillery officer.

'New orders?' he asked feebly.

Hornblower simulated exasperation.

'Get your men away from these guns,' he said. 'Otherwise there may be a deplorable accident.'

'But, monsieur——' The artillery lieutenant pointed down to the quay, and Hornblower now could spare the time to glance back, following the gesture. What he saw made his pounding heart pound harder yet for sheer pleasure. There was the *Nonsuch* against the quay, there was the *Camilla* just coming alongside; but more important yet, there was a big solid block of red coats forming up on the quay. One section with an officer at its head was already heading towards them at a quick step, muskets sloped.

'Send a messenger instantly to the other battery,' said Hornblower, 'to make sure the officer in command there understands.'

'But, monsieur——'

Hornblower stamped his foot with impatience. He could hear the rhythmic tread of the marines behind him, and he gesticulated to them with his hand behind his back. They marched along past him.

'Eyes left!' ordered the subaltern in command, with a smart salute to the French officer. The courtesy took what little wind was left out of the sails of the Frenchman, so that his new protest died on his lips. The marine detachment wheeled to its left round the flank of the battery on the very verge of its dry ditch. Hornblower did not dare take his eyes from the young Frenchman on the parapet, but he sensed what was going on in the rear of the battery. The sally-port there was open, and the marines marched in, still in column of fours, still with their muskets sloped. Now they were in among the guns, pushing the gunners away from their pieces, knocking the smouldering linstocks out of their hands. The young officer was wringing his hands with anxiety.

'All's well that ends well, monsieur,' said Hornblower. 'There might have been a most unpleasant incident.'

Now he could spare a moment to look round. Another marine detachment was off at the quickstep, marching for the other battery. Other parties, seamen and marines, were heading for the other strategic points he had listed in his orders. Brown was coming panting up the slope to be at his side.

The clatter of a horse's hoofs made him turn back again; a mounted French officer was galloping towards them, and reined up amid a shower of flying gravel.

'Get your men away from those guns,' he said

'What is all this?' he demanded. 'What is happening?'

'The news apparently has been delayed in reaching you, monsieur,' said Hornblower. 'The greatest news France has known for twenty years.'

'What is it?'

'Bonaparte rules no more,' said Hornblower. 'Long live the King!'

Those were magic words; words like those of some old-time spell or incantation. No one in the length and breadth of the Empire had dared to say 'Vive le Roi!' since 1792. The mounted officer's jaw dropped for a moment.

'It is false!' he cried, recovering himself. 'The Emperor reigns.'

He looked about him, gathering his reins into his hands, about to ride off.

'Stop him, Brown!' said Hornblower.

Brown took a stride forward, seized the officer's leg in his huge hands, and with a single heave threw him out of the saddle, Hornblower grabbing the bridle in time to prevent the horse from bolting. Brown ran round and extricated the fallen officer's feet from the stirrups.

'I have need of your horse, sir,' said Hornblower.

He got his foot into the stirrup and swung himself awkwardly up into the saddle. The excited brute plunged and almost threw him, but he squirmed back into the saddle, tugged the horse's head round, and then let him go in a wild gallop towards the other battery. His cocked hat flew from his head, his sword and his epaulettes jerked and pounded as he struggled to keep his seat. He tore past the other marine detachment, and heard them cheer him, and then he managed to rein in the frantic horse on the edge of the ditch. Struck with a new idea, he trotted round to the rear of the battery to the main gate.

'Open,' he shouted, 'in the name of the King!'

That was the word of power. There was a clatter of bolts and the upper half of the huge oaken door opened and a couple of startled faces looked out at him. Behind them he saw a musket levelled at him—someone who was a fanatical Bonapartist, probably, or someone too stolid to be taken in by appearances.

'Take that imbecile's musket away from him!' ordered Hornblower. The pressing need of the moment gave an edge to his tone, so that he was obeyed on the instant. 'Now, open the gate.'

He could hear the marines marching up towards him.

'Open the gate!' he roared.

They opened it, and Hornblower walked his horse forward into the battery.

There were twelve vast twenty-four-pounders mounted inside, pointing out through the embrasures down into the harbour. At the back stood the furnace for heating shot with a pyramid of balls beside it. If the two batteries had opened fire nothing hostile could have endured long on the water, and not merely the water but the quay and the waterfront could have been swept clean. And those batteries, with their parapets five feet thick and eight feet high, and their dry ditches, ten feet deep cut square in the solid rock, could never have been stormed without regular siege methods. The bewildered gunners stared at him, and at the red-coated marines who came marching in behind him. A callow subaltern approached him.

'I do not understand this, sir,' he said. 'Who are you, and why did you say what you did?'

The subaltern could not bring himself to utter the word 'King'; it was a word that was taboo—he was like some old maid posing a delicate question to a doctor. Hornblower smiled at him, using all his self-control to conceal his exultation, for it would never do to triumph too openly.

'This is the beginning of a new age for France,' he said.

The sound of music came to his ears. Hornblower dismounted and left his horse free, and ran up the steps cut in the back of the parapet, the subaltern following. Standing on the top of the parapet with the vast arms of the semaphore over their heads, the whole panorama of the port was open to them; the squadron lying against the quay, the detachments of the landing party, red-coated or white-shirted, on the march hither and thither, and, on the quay itself, the marine band striding up towards the town, the drums thundering and the bugles braying, the red coats and the white crossbelts and the glittering instruments making a brave spectacle. That had been Hornblower's crowning idea; nothing would be more likely to convince a wavering garrison that he came in peace than a band calmly playing selections as it marched in.

The harbour defences were secured now; he had carried out his part of the scheme. Whatever had happened to Lebrun, the squadron was not in serious danger; if the main garrison had refused to be seduced, and turned against him, he could spike the batteries' guns, blow up the magazines, and warp his ships out almost at leisure, taking with him whatever prisoners and booty he could lay his hands on. The awkward moment had been when the guard-boat had fired its gun—firing is infectious. But the fact of only one shot being fired, the delay, the mist, had made the inexperienced officer in command of the batteries wait for orders, giving him time to use his personal influence. It was evident already that part of Lebrun's scheme, at least, had been successful. Lebrun had not made up his mind, at the time of his leaving the *Flame,* whether it would be a banquet or a council of war to

which he would summon the senior officers, but whichever
it was he had clearly succeeded in depriving the harbour
defences of all direction. Apparently, too, Lebrun's story that
a blockade runner was expected to arrive during the night,
and his request that the harbour defences should hold their
fire until certain as to the identity of any ship entering the port,
had had their effect as well—the man was a born intriguer;
but Hornblower still did not know whether the rest of his
coup d'état had succeeded. This was no time for delay; there
were too many examples in history of promising enterprises
brought to naught after a good beginning solely because
someone did not push on at the psychological moment.

He wanted to make a bold push, but at the same time he
felt nervous about involving his landing party in the narrow
streets of the town without some assurance of a friendly
reception there. Here came Howard, riding gracefully; apparently he, too, had been able to procure himself a horse.

'Any orders, sir?' Howard asked. Two midshipmen and
Brown were running beside him, the midshipmen presumably
to act as messengers.

'Not yet,' answered Hornblower, fuming inwardly with
anxiety while trying to appear calm.

'Your hat, sir,' said the admirable Brown, who had picked
the thing up while on his way from the other battery.

Here came a horseman at a gallop, a white band on his
arm, a white handkerchief fluttering in his hand. He reined
in when he saw Hornblower's gold lace.

'You are Monsieur—Monsieur——' he began.

'Hornblower.' No Frenchman had ever been able to
pronounce that name.

'From Baron Momas, sir. The citadel is secure. He is
about to descend into the main square.'

'The soldiers in the barracks?'

'They are tranquil.'

'The main guard at the gate?'

'I do not know, sir.'

'Howard, take your reserve. March for the gate as hard as you can. This man will go with you to explain to the guard. If they will not come over, let them desert. They can march out into the open country—it will not matter. No bloodshed if you can help it, but make sure of the gate.'

'Aye aye, sir.'

Hornblower explained to the Frenchman what he had said.

'Brown, come with me. I shall be in the main square if needed, Howard.'

It was not much of a procession Howard was able to form, two score marines and seamen, but the band blared out as best it could as Hornblower marched triumphantly up the street. The people on the route looked at them, curious or sullen or merely indifferent, but there was no sign of active resentment. In the Place de l'Hôtel de Ville there was far more bustle and life. Numerous men sat their horses there; a detachment of police, drawn up in line, gave an appearance of respectability to the proceedings. But what caught the eye was the multitude of white emblems. There were white cockades in the hats of the gendarmes, and the mounted officials wore white scarves or armbands. White flags—bed sheets, apparently—hung from most of the windows. For the first time in more than twenty years the Bourbon white was being flaunted on the soil of France. A fat man on foot, a white sash round his belly where (Hornblower guessed) yesterday he had worn the tricolour, hurried towards him as he rode in. Hornblower signalled frantically to the band to stop, and scrambled down from the saddle, handing the reins to Brown as he advanced towards the man he guessed to be Momas.

'Our friend,' said Momas, his arms outspread. 'Our ally!'

Hornblower allowed himself to be embraced—even at that moment he wondered what the leathernecks behind him would think about the sight of a commodore being kissed by a fat Frenchman—and then saluted the rest of the Mayor's staff as they came to greet him. Lebrun was at their head, grinning.

'A great moment, sir,' said the Mayor.

'A great moment indeed, Monsieur le Baron.'

The Mayor waved his hand towards the flagstaff that stood outside the Mairie.

'The ceremony is about to take place,' he said.

Lebrun was at his side with a paper, and Momas took it and mounted the steps at the foot of the flagstaff. He inflated his lungs and began to read at the top of his voice. It was curious how the French love of legal forms and appearances showed itself even here, at this moment of treason; the proclamation was studded with archaisms and seemed interminable in its prolixity. It mentioned the misdeeds of the usurper, Napoleon Bonaparte, it denounced all his pretensions to sovereignty, it disclaimed all allegiance to him. Instead it declared that all Frenchmen voluntarily recognized the unbroken reign of His Most Christian Majesty, Louis XVIII, King of France and Navarre. At those resounding words the men at the foot of the flagstaff hauled busily at the halliards, and the white standard of the Bourbons soared up the mast.

Hornblower replaced his hat and stiffly saluted the white flag. Now it was time, and high time, to start organizing the defence of the town against Bonaparte's wrath.

The Duc d'Angoulême

THE demands upon the time and energy of the Governor of Le Havre were enormous; Hornblower sighed as he looked at the papers stacked on his desk. There was so much to do; Saxton, the engineer officer just arrived from England, was clamouring to build a new battery to cover the defences of the Rouen Gate. There was the question of unloading the food ships which Whitehall had sent him. There was the question of policing the streets. Old personal scores had been wiped out, Hornblower guessed, in the one or two murders of prominent Bonapartists, and there had already been some attempt at reprisal by secret assassination. He could run no risk, now that the city was under control, of allowing it to be divided against itself. The court martial was in progress of those mutineers of the *Flame* whom he had not pardoned. In every case the sentence would be death, inevitably, and there was food for thought in that. He was Commodore of the British Squadron as well as Governor of Le Havre, and there was all the manifold business of the squadron to be attended to. He must decide about——

Hornblower was already walking up and down. This vast room in the Hôtel de Ville was far better adapted for walking in than was any quarter-deck. He had had two weeks now to adapt himself to the absence of fresh air and wide horizons; his head was bent on his breast and his hands were clasped behind him as he paced, forming the decisions that were demanded of him. It may have been a great honour to be entrusted with the governorship of Le Havre, to head the attack upon Bonaparte, but it was onerous.

Here came another interruption; an elderly officer in a dark-green uniform waving a paper in his hand. This was— what was his name again?—Hau, a captain in the 60th Rifles. Nobody knew quite what his nationality was by this time; maybe he did not know himself. He apparently, before the French Revolution, had been a Court official of one of the innumerable little states on the French side of the Rhine.

'The Foreign Office bag is in, sir,' said Hau, 'and this despatch was marked "urgent." '

Hornblower took his mind from the problem of nominating a new *juge de paix* to deal with the new problem.

'They're sending us a prince,' said Hornblower, having read the letter.

'Which one, sir?' asked Hau, with keen and immediate interest.

'The Duc d'Angoulême.'

'Eventual heir of the Bourbon line,' said Hau, judiciously. 'Eldest son of the Comte d'Artois, Louis' brother. By his mother he descends from the House of Savoy. And he married Marie Thérèse, the Prisoner of the Temple, daughter of the martyred Louis XVI. A good choice. He must be aged about forty now.'

Hornblower wondered vaguely what use a royal prince would be to him. It might sometimes be a convenience to have a figurehead, but he could foresee—Hornblower was labouring under all the burden of disillusionment—that the Duke's presence would much more often involve him in additional and unprofitable labours.

'He will arrive to-morrow if the wind is fair,' said Hau.

'And it is,' said Hornblower, looking out of the window at

the flagstaff, where fluttered, side by side, the Union flag of England and the white flag of the Bourbons.

'He must be received with all the solemnity the occasion demands,' said Hau. 'A Bourbon prince setting foot on French soil for the first time in twenty years. At the quay he must be greeted by all the authorities. A royal salute. A procession to the church. Te Deum to be sung there. A procession to the Hôtel de Ville, and there a grand reception.'

'That is all your business,' said Hornblower.

The bitter cold of winter still persisted unbroken. Down on the quay, where Hornblower waited while the frigate bearing the Duke was being warped in, a cutting north-easterly wind was blowing, which pierced through the heavy cloak he was wearing. He watched with professional interest the warping in of the frigate; he heard the clanking of the windlass and the sharp orders of the officers. A brow was thrown from the gangway to the quay, and here came the Duke, a tall, stiff man in a Hussar uniform, a blue ribbon across his chest. In the ship the pipes of the bosun's mates twittered in a long call, the marines presented arms, the officers saluted.

'Step forward to greet His Royal Highness, sir,' prompted Hau at Hornblower's elbow.

There was a magic mid-point in the brow over which the Duke was walking; as he passed it he crossed from the British ship to the soil of France. Down came the French royal standard from the frigate's masthead. The pipes died away in one last ecstatic wail. The massed bands burst out in a triumphal march, the salutes began to roar, seamen and soldiers of the guard of honour presented arms after the fashion of two services and two nations. Hornblower found himself stepping forward, laying his cocked hat across his breast in the gesture he had painfully rehearsed under Hau's guidance that morning, and bowing to the representative of His Most Christian Majesty.

'Sir 'Oratio,' said the Duke cordially—for all his lifetime in exile apparently he still had a Frenchman's difficulty in dealing with aspirates. He looked round him. 'France, beautiful France.'

Anything less beautiful than the waterfront of Le Havre with a nor'easter blowing Hornblower could not imagine, but perhaps the Duke meant it, and, anyway, the words would sound well to posterity.

Out of the tail of his eye Hornblower saw the massed dignitaries behind him straightening themselves up from their concerted bow, their hats still across their stomachs.

'Cover yourselves, gentlemen, I beg of you,' said the Duke, and the grey hairs and the bald heads disappeared as the dignitaries gratefully shielded themselves from the wintry wind.

Hornblower turned and beckoned for the horses to be led up; the equerry hastened to hold the stirrup, and the Duke swung himself into the saddle, a born horseman like all his family. Hornblower mounted the quiet horse he had reserved for himself, and the others followed his example.

They rode up the Rue de Paris, scourged by the wind, and all round the grand square before dismounting again outside the Hôtel de Ville. The cheers of the people seemed thin and spiritless, and the wave of the hand or the lifting of the hat with which the Duke acknowledged them seemed wooden and mechanical. His Royal Highness possessed much of that stoical power to endure hardship in public without flinching which royalty must always display, but seemingly it had been acquired at the cost of making him silent and reserved.

Hornblower watched him down the length of the great hall

in the Hôtel de Ville—freezing cold, too, despite the fires
which blazed at either end—as he greeted in turn the local
dignitaries and their wives who were led up to him. The
mechanical smile, the apt but formal phrase of greeting, the
carefully graded courtesies, from the inclination of the head
to the slight bow; all these indicated the care taken in his
schooling. And clustered behind him and at his side were
his advisers, the *émigré* nobles he had brought with him,
Momas and Lebrun representing France since the revolution,
Hau watching over British interests.

Someone was twitching at Hornblower's sleeve; there
seemed to be warning in the touch, and he turned slowly to
find Brown, soberly dressed in his best clothes, at his elbow.

'Colonel Dobbs sent me in to you, sir,' said Brown. 'Despatch come in, sir, and Colonel Dobbs says he'd like you to
see it, sir.'

'I'll come in a moment,' said Hornblower.

Brown sidled away; despite his bulk and height, he could
be very unobtrusive when he wished. Hornblower waited long
enough to make it appear unlikely that his own departure
was connected with Brown's message, and then made his way
out past the sentries at the door. He strode up the stairs two
at a time to his office, where the red-coated marine colonel
stood waiting for him.

'They're on their way at last, sir,' said Dobbs, handing over
the message for Hornblower to read.

It was a long, narrow strip of paper, yet narrow as it was,
it had been longitudinally folded as well as crossways; such a
peculiar letter that Hornblower looked a question at Dobbs
before reading it.

'It was folded up in a button on the messenger's coat, sir,'
explained Dobbs. 'From an agent in Paris.'

Plenty of people in high position, Hornblower knew, were

betraying their Imperial master, selling military and political secrets either for present gain or for future advancement.

'The messenger left Paris yesterday,' said Dobbs. 'He rode post to Honfleur, and crossed the river after dark to-day.'

The message was written by someone who knew his business.

This morning, it said, *siege artillery left the artillery park at Sablons by river, going downstream. It included the 107th Regiment of Artillery. The guns were 24-pounders, and I believe there were 24 of them. Three companies of sappers and a company of miners were attached. It is said that General Quiot will command. I do not know what other forces he will have.*

There was no signature, and the handwriting was disguised. 'Is this genuine?' asked Hornblower.

'Yes, sir. Harrison says so. And it agrees with those other reports we've been receiving from Rouen.'

So Bonaparte, locked in a death struggle in eastern France with the Russians and the Prussians and the Austrians, fighting for his life in the south against Wellington, had yet contrived to scrape together a force to counter the new menace in the north. There could be no doubt against whom the siege artillery was destined to be used. Down the Seine from Paris his only enemies were the rebels in Le Havre; the presence of sappers and miners was a clear proof that a siege was intended, and that the guns were not merely intended to strengthen some land fortification. And Quiot had some two divisions mustering in Rouen.

The Seine offered Bonaparte every convenience for striking a blow at Le Havre. By water the heavy guns could be moved far more quickly than by road, especially by winter roads; even the troops, packed into barges, would travel faster than on their own feet. Night and day those barges would be towed downstream—by now they must already be nearing Rouen. It could be no more than a matter of a few days before Quiot closed in on the city.

Hornblower had forgotten the presence of the marine colonel; he looked past him into vacancy. It was time for the rebellion to cease the defensive, and to take the offensive, however limited its means, however powerful the enemy. Something must be done, something must be dared. He could not bear the thought of cowering behind the fortifications of Le Havre, like a rabbit in its burrow, waiting for Quiot and his sappers to come and ferret him out.

'Let me see that map again,' he said to Dobbs. 'How are the tides now? You don't know? Then find out, man, immediately. And I want a report on the roads between here and Rouen. Brown! Go and get Captain Bush out of the reception.'

He was still making plans and giving provisional orders, when Hau came into the room.

'The reception is ending, sir,' said Hau. 'His Royal Highness is about to retire.'

Hornblower cast one more look at the map of the lower Seine spread before him; his brain was seething, with calculations regarding tides and road distances.

'Oh, very well,' he said. 'I'll come for five minutes.'

Success and Tragedy at Caudebec

THE murky winter day was giving place to murky night. There was little of the grey winter afternoon left as Hornblower stood on the quay watching the boats make ready. It was already dark enough and misty enough for the preparations to be invisible to anyone outside the town, whatever point of vantage he might have chosen for himself. So it was safe for the seamen and the marines to begin to man the boats; it was only an hour before the flood tide should begin, and no moment of the tide ought to be wasted.

This was another of the penalties of success; that he should have to stand here and watch others set off on an expedition that he would have loved to head. But the Governor of Le Havre, the Commodore, could not possibly risk his life and liberty with a petty sortie; the force he was sending out, crammed into half a dozen ships' longboats, was so small that he was hardly justified in putting a post captain in command.

Bush came stumping up to him, the thump of his wooden leg on the cobbles alternating with the flatter sound of his one shoe.

'No further orders, sir?' asked Bush.

'No, none. I only have to wish you the best of good fortune now,' said Hornblower.

He put out his hand, and Bush took it—amazing how Bush's hand remained hard and horny as if he still had to haul on braces and halliards. Bush's frank blue eyes looked into his.

'Thank you, sir,' said Bush, and then, after a moment's hesitation, 'Don't you go worrying about us, sir.'

'I won't worry with you in command, Bush.'

There was some truth in that. In all these years of close association Bush had learned his methods, and could be relied upon to execute a plan intelligently. Bush knew as well as he did now the value of surprise, the importance of striking swiftly and suddenly and unexpectedly, the necessity for close co-operation between all parts of the force.

The *Nonsuch's* longboat was against the quay, and a detachment of marines was marching down into it. They sat stiff and awkward on the thwarts, their muskets pointing skywards between their knees, while the seamen held the boat off.

'All ready, sir?' piped up a voice from the sternsheets.

'Good-bye, Bush,' said Hornblower.

'Good-bye, sir.'

Bush's powerful arms swung him down into the longboat with no difficulty despite his wooden leg.

'Shove off.'

The boat pushed out from the quay; two other boats left the quay as well. There was still just enough light to see the rest of the flotilla pull away from the sides of the ships moored in the harbour. The sound of the orders came to Hornblower's ears across the water.

'Give way.'

Bush's boat swung round and headed the procession out into the river, and the night swallowed it. Yet Hornblower stood looking after them into the blackness for some time before he turned away. There could be no doubt at all, having regard to the state of the roads, and the reports of the spies, that Quiot would bring his siege-train as far as Caudebec by water—barges would carry his vast twenty-four-pounders fifty miles in a day, while over those muddy surfaces they would hardly move fifty miles in a week. At Caudebec there was an *estacade* with facilities for dealing with large cargoes. Quiot's advanced guards at Lillebonne and Bolbec would cover the unloading—so he would think. There was a good chance that boats, coming up the river in the darkness swiftly with the tide, might arrive unobserved at the *estacade*. The landing party could burn and destroy to their hearts' content in that case. Most likely Bonaparte's troops, which had conquered the land world, would not think of the possibility of an amphibious expedition striking by water round their flank; and even if they did think of it there was more than a chance that the expedition, moving rapidly on the tide, would break through the defence in the darkness as far as the barges. But though it was easy enough to form these comforting conclusions, it was not so easy to see the boats go off in the darkness like this. Hornblower turned away from the quay and began to walk up the dark Rue de Paris to the Hôtel de Ville.

In his bedroom there was a privacy to be obtained which he could not hope for elsewhere. He dismissed Brown as soon as the latter had lighted the candles in the stick on the night table at the bedhead, and with a grateful sigh he stretched himself out on the bed, careless of his uniform. He rose again to get his boat-cloak and spread it over himself, for the room was dank and cold despite the fire in the grate. Then at last he could take the newspaper from the top of the pile at the bedhead, and set himself to read seriously the marked passages at which previously he had merely glanced.

If the Press was, as it claimed to be, the voice of the people, then the British public most strongly approved of him and his recent actions. Here was *The Times* running over with praise for his handling of the situation in the Bay of the Seine. The measures he had taken to make it impossible for the mutineers to take the *Flame* in to the French authorities were described as 'a masterpiece of the ingenuity and skill which we have come to expect of this brilliant officer.' Here was the *Morning Chronicle* expatiating on his capture of the *Flame* across the decks of the *Bonne Celestine*. There was only one example in history of a similar feat—Nelson's capture of the *San Josef* at Cape St Vincent. Hornblower's eyebrows rose as he read. The comparison was quite absurd.

He flung the *Morning Chronicle* aside and took up the *Anti Gallican*. The writer here gloated over the fate of the mutineers. He exulted over the death of Nathaniel Sweet, laying special stress on the fact that he had died at Hornblower's own hands. He went on to hope that Sweet's accessories in the horrible crime of mutiny would shortly meet the fate they deserved, and he hoped that the happy issue of Hornblower's recapture of the *Flame* would not be allowed to serve as an excuse for mercy or sentimental considerations. Hornblower, with twenty sentences of death awaiting his signature, felt his nausea renewed. This writer in the *Anti Gallican* did not know what death was.

A later number of *The Times* discussed the capture of Le Havre. *The Times* expected Bonaparte's dominion, which had endured all these years, to melt away in the next few days. The crossing of the Rhine, the fall of Le Havre, the declaration of Bordeaux in favour of the Bourbons, made the writer certain that Bonaparte would be dethroned immediately. Yet Bonaparte with a solid army was still striking back at his enemies to-day. No one could foresee an immediate end to the war save this inky scribbler safe in some dusty office in Printing House Square.

He had hardly finished the pile of newspapers when he noticed the bed jar slightly under him and the candle-flames flicker for a moment. He paid almost no attention to the phenomenon—it might have been a heavy gun being fired, although he had not heard the explosion—but a few seconds later he heard the bedroom door stealthily opened. He looked up to see Brown peering round the corner at him to see if he were asleep.

'What do you want?' he snapped. His ill-temper was so obvious that even Brown hesitated to speak.

'Out with it,' snarled Hornblower. 'Why am I being disturbed contrary to my orders?'

Howard and Dobbs made their appearance behind Brown; it was to their credit that they were willing not merely to take the responsibility but to receive the first impact of the wrath of the Commodore.

'There's been an explosion, sir,' said Howard. 'We saw

the flash of it in the sky, east by north of here—I took the bearing. That could be at Caudebec.'

'We felt the jar, sir,' said Dobbs. 'But there was no sound —too far away. A big explosion to shake us here and yet be unheard.'

That meant, almost for certain, that Bush had been successful. He must have captured the French powder-barges and blown them up. A thousand rounds for each of twenty-four twenty-four pounders—the minimum for a siege; eight pounds of powder for each round. That would be eight times twenty-four thousand. That would be nearly two hundred thousand pounds. That would be almost a hundred tons. A hundred tons of gunpowder would make a fair explosion. Having computed his calculation, Hornblower refocused his eyes on Dobbs and Howard; until then he had looked at them without seeing them. Brown had tactfully slipped out from this council of his betters.

'Well?' said Hornblower.

'We thought you would like to know about it, sir,' said Dobbs, lamely.

'Quite right,' said Hornblower, and held up his newspaper between them again. Then he pulled it down again just long enough to say, 'Thank you.'

The fact that he had not taken off his clothes told Brown and Dobbs and Howard at dawn that Hornblower had not been as composed and self-confident as he had tried to appear, but not one of them was foolish enough to comment on the fact. Brown merely opened the curtain and made his report.

'Day just breaking, sir. Cold morning with a bit o' fog. The last o' the ebb, sir, and no news as yet of Captain Bush an' the flotilla.'

'Right,' said Hornblower, getting stiffly to his feet. He yawned and felt his bristling cheeks. He wished he knew how Bush had succeeded. He wished he did not feel so un-washed and unclean. He wanted his breakfast, but he wanted news of Bush even more. He was still deadly tired.

'Get me a bath, Brown. Make it ready while I shave.'

'Aye aye, sir.'

Hornblower stripped off his clothes and proceeded to shave himself at the wash-hand-stand in the corner of the room. Brown and a marine private came in carrying the bath and put it on the floor near him; it took a little while to compound the mixture in the right proportion so as to get the tempera-ture suitable. Hornblower stepped into it and sank down with a sigh of satisfaction—an immense amount of water poured over the sides, displaced by his body, but he did not care. He closed his eyes.

'Sir!'

Howard's voice caused him to reopen them.

'Two boats are in sight coming down the estuary, sir. Only two.'

Bush had taken seven boats with him to Caudebec. Hornblower could only wait for Howard to finish his report.

'One of 'em's *Camilla's* launch, sir. I can recognize her through the glass. I don't think the other is from *Nonsuch*, but I can't be sure.'

'Very good, Captain. I'll join you in a moment.'

Ruin and destruction; five boats lost out of seven—and Bush lost too, seemingly. The destruction of the French siege-train—if it were destroyed—would be well worth the loss of the whole flotilla, to someone who could coldly balance profit and loss. But Bush gone! Hornblower could not bear the thought of it. He dressed hurriedly, and at every moment his fears and his sorrow on account of Bush increased—the first shock had not been nearly as severe as this growing realiza-tion of his bereavement. He came out into the ante-room.

'One boat's coming into the quay, sir. I'll have the officer reporting here in fifteen minutes,' said Howard.

Brown was across the room at the far door. Now, if ever, Hornblower had the opportunity—his unaccountable brain recognized it at this moment—to show himself a man of iron. All he had to do was to say 'My breakfast, Brown,' and sit down and eat it. But he could not pose, faced as he was by the possibility of Bush's death. It was all very well to do those things when it was merely a battle that lay before him, but this was the loss of his dearest friend. Brown must have read the expression on his face, for he withdrew without making any suggestion about breakfast. Hornblower stood undecided.

'I have the court-martial verdicts here for confirmation, sir,' said Howard, calling his attention to a mass of papers.

Hornblower sat down and picked one up, looked at it unseeing, and put it down again.

'I'll deal with that later on,' he said.

'Cider's begun coming into the city from the country in great quantity, sir, now that the farmers have found it's a good market,' said Dobbs. 'Drunkenness among the men's increasing. Can we——?'

'I'll leave it to your judgment,' said Hornblower. 'Now. What is it you want to do?'

'I would submit, sir, that——'

The discussion lasted a few minutes. It led naturally to the vexed question of an established rate of exchange for British and French currency. But it could not dull the gnawing anxiety about Bush.

'Where the hell's that officer?' said Howard, petulantly pushing back his chair and going out of the room. He was back almost immediately.

'Mr Livingstone, sir,' he said. 'Third of *Camilla*.'

A middle-aged lieutenant, steady and reliable enough to

outward appearance; Hornblower looked him over carefully
as he came into the room.

'Make your report, please.'

'We went up the river without incident, sir. *Flame's* boat
went aground but was refloated directly. We could see the
lights of Caudebec before we were challenged from the
bank—we were just rounding the bend, then. Cap'n Bush's
longboat was leading, sir.'

'Where was your boat?'

'Last in the line, sir. We went on without replying, as our
orders said. I could see two barges anchored in midstream,
an' clusters of others against the bank. I put the tiller over
and ran beside the one farthest downstream, as my orders
said, sir. There was a lot of musketry fire higher up, but only
a few Frenchies where we were, an' we chased 'em away.
On the bank where we were there were two twenty-four-
pounders on travelling carriages. I had 'em spiked, and then
we levered them off the bank into the river. One fell on to
the barge underneath an' went through it, sir. It sank alongside my launch, deck just level with the water; just before
the turn of the tide, that was. Don't know what she carried,
sir, but I think she was light, judging by the height she rode
out of the water when I boarded her. Her hatches were open.'

'Yes?'

'Then I led my party along the bank as ordered, sir. There
was a lot of shot there, just landed from the next barge. The
barge was only half unloaded. So I left a party to scuttle the
barge and roll the shot into the river, an' went on myself
with about fifteen men, sir. *Flame's* boat's crew was there,
an' the party they were fighting against ran away when we
came on their flank. There were guns on shore and guns still
in the barges, sir. We spiked 'em all, threw the ones that had
been landed into the river, and scuttled the barges. There

was no powder, sir. My orders were to blow the trunnions off the guns if I could, but I couldn't.'

'I understand.'

Guns spiked and pitched into the slime at the bottom of a rapid tidal river would be out of action for some time, even though it would have been better to blow off their trunnions and disable them permanently. And the shot at the bottom of the river would be difficult to recover. Hornblower could picture so well in his mind the fierce and bloody little struggle in the dark on the river bank.

'Just then we heard drums beating, sir, and a whole lot of soldiers came bearing down on us. A battalion of infantry, I should think it was—I think we had only been engaged up to then with the gunners an' sappers. My orders were to withdraw if opposed in force, so we ran back to the boats. We'd just shoved off and the soldiers were firing at us from the banks when the explosion came.'

Livingstone paused. His unshaven face was grey with fatigue, and when he mentioned the explosion his expression changed to one of helplessness.

'It was the powder-barges higher up the river, sir. I don't know who set them off. Maybe it was a shot from the shore. Maybe Cap'n Bush, sir——'

'You had not been in touch with Captain Bush since the attack began?'

'No, sir. He was at the other end of the line to me, and the barges were in two groups against the bank. I attacked one, an' Cap'n Bush attacked the other.'

'I understand. Go on about the explosion.'

'It was a big one, sir. It threw us all down. A big wave came an' swamped us, filled us to the gunnels, sir. I think we touched the bottom of the river, sir, after that wave went by. A bit of flying wreckage hit *Flame's* boat. Gibbons, master's mate, was killed an' the boat smashed. We picked up the survivors while we bailed out. Nobody was firing at us from the bank any more, so I waited. It was just the top of the tide, sir. Presently two boats came down to us, *Camilla's* second launch and the fishing-boat that the marines manned. We waited, but we could not see anything of *Nonsuch's* boats. Mr Hake of the marines told me that Cap'n Bush an' the other three boats were all alongside the powder-barges when the explosion happened. Perhaps a shot went into the cargo, sir. Then they began to open fire on us from the bank again, and as senior officer I gave the order to retire.'

'Most likely you did right, Mr Livingstone. And then?'

'At the next bend they opened fire on us with field-pieces, sir. Their practice was bad in the dark, sir, but they hit and sank our second launch with almost their last shot, and we lost several more men—the current was running fast by then.'

That was clearly the end of Livingstone's story, but Hornblower could not dismiss him without one more word.

'But Captain Bush, Mr Livingstone? Can't you tell me any more about him?'

'No, sir. I'm sorry, sir. We didn't pick up a single survivor from the *Nonsuch's* boats. Not one.'

'Oh, very well then, Mr Livingstone. You had better go and get some rest. I think you did very well.'

'Let me have your report in writing and list of casualties before the end of the day, Mr Livingstone,' interposed Dobbs —as Assistant-Adjutant-General he lived in an atmosphere of reports and lists of casualties.

'Aye aye, sir.'

Livingstone withdrew, and the door had hardly closed upon him before Hornblower regretted having let him go with such chary words of commendation. The operation had been brilliantly successful. Deprived of his siege-train and munitions, Quiot would not be able to besiege Le Havre, and it would probably be a long time before Bonaparte's War Ministry in Paris could scrape together another train. But the loss of Bush coloured all Hornblower's thoughts. He found himself wishing that he had never conceived the plan —he would rather have stood a siege here in Le Havre and have Bush alive at his side. It was hard to think of a world without Bush in it, of a future where he would never, never see Bush again. People would think the loss of a captain and a hundred and fifty men a small price to pay for robbing Quiot of all his offensive power, but people did not understand.

The Fruits of Victory

HORNBLOWER'S breakfast was interrupted a fortnight later by a thump at the door. It was Dobbs.

'Despatch from the army, sir. The Frogs have gone.'

'Gone?'

'Up-stick and away, sir. Quiot marched for Paris last night. There's not a French soldier in Rouen.'

The report that Hornblower took from Dobbs' hand merely repeated in more formal language what Dobbs had said. Bonaparte must be desperate for troops to defend his capital; by recalling Quiot he had left all Normandy exposed to the invader.

'We must follow him up,' said Hornblower to himself, and then to Dobbs, 'Tell Howard—no I'll come myself.'

In the office he read the reconnaissance report again. It stated unequivocally that no contact could be made with any Imperial troops whatever, and that prominent citizens of Rouen, escaping from the town, assured the outposts that not a Bonapartist soldier remained there. Rouen was his for the taking, and obviously the tendency to desert Bonaparte and join the Bourbons was becoming more and more marked. Every day the number of people who came into Le Havre by road or by boat to make their submission to the Duke grew larger and larger.

'*Vive le Roi!*' was what they called out as they neared the sentries. 'Long live the King!'

That was the password which marked the Bourbonist—no Bonapartist, no Jacobin, no republican would soil his lips with those words. And the number of deserters and refractory conscripts who came pouring in was growing enormous. It might be thought possible that a Bourbonist army could be built up from this material, but the attempt was a failure from the start. Those runaways objected not merely to fighting for Bonaparte, but to fighting at all. The Royalist army which Angoulême had been sent here to organize still numbered less than a thousand men, and it was fortunate for Hornblower that a force of militia and two regiments of yeomanry had just arrived from England to strengthen his command. Another arrival from England was the Duchess of Angoulême, who had come to join her husband at the head of the Royalist revolt.

But Rouen awaited a conqueror, nevertheless. Hornblower's militia brigade could tramp the miry roads to the city, and he and Angoulême could get into carriages and drive after them. A fresh idea struck him. In eastern France the allied monarchs were riding every few days into some new captured town. It was in his power to escort Angoulême into Rouen in more spectacular fashion, demonstrating at the same time the long arm of England's sea power, and rubbing in the lesson that it was England's naval strength which had turned the balance of the war. The wind was westerly; he was a little vague about the state of the tide, but he could wait until it should serve.

'Captain Howard,' he said, looking up, 'warn *Flame* and *Porta Coeli* to be ready to get under way. I shall take the Duke and Duchess up to Rouen by water. And their whole suite. Warn the captains to make preparations for their reception and accommodation. Send me Hau to settle the details. Colonel Dobbs, would you be interested in a little yachting trip?'

It seemed indeed like a yachting trip next morning, when they gathered on the quarter-deck of the *Porta Coeli,* a group of men in brilliant uniforms and women in gay dresses. *Porta Coeli* had already warped away from the quay, from which they rowed out to her, and Freeman, at a nod from Hornblower, had only to bellow the orders for sail to be set and the anchor hove in for them to start up the broad estuary. The sun was shining with the full promise of spring, the wavelets gleamed and danced. Down below decks, Hornblower could guess from the sounds, there was trouble and toil, while they were still trying to rig accommodation for the royal party, but here by the taffrail all was laughter and expectancy. And it was heavenly to tread a deck again, to feel the wind on his cheeks, to look aft and see *Flame* under all fore-and-aft sail in her station astern, to have the white ensign overhead and his broad pendant hoisted, even though the Bourbon white and gold flew beside it.

The Duke and Duchess condescended to step to his side and engage him in conversation. They were bowling up the channel at a full eight knots, faster than if they had gone in carriages, but of course when the river began to narrow and to wind it might be a different story. The southern shore came northward to meet them, the flat green shore becoming more and more defined, until in a flash, as it seemed, they were out of the estuary and between the banks of the river, leaving Quillebœuf behind and opening up the long reach that led to Caudebec, the left bank green pasture-land studded with fat farms, the right bank lofty and wooded. Over went the helm, the sheets were hauled in. But with the wind tending to funnel up the valley it was still well over their quarter, and with the racing tide behind them they fairly tore along the river. Luncheon was announced, and the party trooped below, the women squealing at the lowness of the decks and the difficulty

of the companion. Bulkheads had been ripped out and replaced to make ample room for royalty—Hornblower guessed
that half the crew would be sleeping on deck in consequence
of the presence of the Duke and Duchess. The royal servants,
assisted by the wardroom stewards—the former as embar-
rassed by their surroundings as the latter by the company
on whom they had to wait—began to serve the food, but
luncheon had hardly begun when Freeman came in to
whisper to Hornblower as he sat between the Duchess and
the *dame d'honneur*.

'Caudebec in sight, sir,' whispered Freeman; Hornblower
had left orders to be told when this happened.

With an apology to the Duchess and a bow to the Duke,
Hornblower slipped unobtrusively out of the room; the
etiquette of royalty even covered events on shipboard, and
sailors could come and go with little ceremony if the management of the vessel demanded it. Caudebec was in sight at the
top of the reach, and they were approaching it fast, so that it
was only a matter of minutes before there was no need for the
glass that Hornblower trained on the little town. The damage
caused by the explosion which had cost Bush's life was very
obvious. Every house had been cut off short six or eight feet
from the ground; the massive church had withstood the shock
save that most of its roof had been stripped off and its windows
blown in. The long wooden quay was in ruins, and a few
stumps of blackened wrecks showed above water-level beside
it. A single cannon—a twenty-four-pounder on a travelling
carriage—stood on the river bank above the quay, all that
remained of Quiot's siege-train. A few people were to be seen;
they stood staring at the two men-o'-war brigs sailing along
the river past them.

'A nasty sight, sir,' said Freeman beside him.

'Yes,' said Hornblower.

This was where Bush died; Hornblower stood silent in tribute to his friend. When the war was over he would erect a little monument on the river bank there above the quay. He could wish that the ruined town would never be rebuilt; that would be the most striking monument to his friend's memory—that or a pyramid of skulls.

Here was Hau beside him now.

'Monseigneur wishes to know,' he said, 'whether your business on deck is very urgent. His Royal Highness has a toast to propose, and wishes that you could join in it.'

'I'll come,' said Hornblower.

He took a last glance aft at Caudebec, vanishing round the bend, and hurried below. The big extemporized cabin was parti-coloured with sunlight coming in through the open ports. Angoulême caught sight of him as he entered, and rose to his feet, crouching under the low deck-beams.

'To His Royal Highness the Prince Regent!' he said, lifting his glass. The toast was drunk, and everyone looked to Hornblower for the proper response.

'His Most Christian Majesty!' said Hornblower, and when the ceremony was completed raised his glass again.

'His most Christian Majesty's Regent in Normandy, Monseigneur His Royal Highness the Duke d'Angoulême!'

The toast was drunk amid a roar of acclamation. There was something dramatic and painful about being down here below decks drinking toasts while an Empire was falling in ruins outside. Hornblower heard Freeman roar a fresh order on deck, and was consumed with restlessness. Down here it was like being with a nursery party of children, enjoying themselves while the adults attended to the management of the world. He made his apologetic bow again and slipped out to go on deck.

The *Porta Coeli* was as close-hauled as she would lie,

almost closer. Her sails were shivering and her motion slug-
gish, and the bend in the river that would give her relief was
a full half-mile farther ahead. Freeman looked up at the
flapping sails and shook his head.

'You'll have to club-haul her, Mr Freeman,' said Hornblower. To tack in that narrow channel, even with the tide
behind them, would be too tricky an operation altogether.

'Aye aye, sir,' said Freeman.

He stood for a second judging his distances; the hands at
the sheets, in no doubt about the delicacy of the ensuing
manœuvres, waiting keyed up for the rapid succession of
orders that would follow. Filling the sails for a moment
gave them plenty of way again, although it brought them
perilously close to the leeward shore. Then in came the
sheets, over went the helm, and the *Porta Coeli* snatched a
few yards into the wind, losing most of her way in the process.
Then out went the sheets, up came the helm a trifle, and she
gathered way again, close-hauled yet edging down perceptibly
towards the lee shore.

'Well done,' said Hornblower. He wanted to add a word
of advice to the effect that it would be as well not to leave it
so late next time, but he glanced at Freeman sizing up the
distances and decided it was unnecessary. Freeman wanted
none of the brig's way lost this time. The moment the sails
flapped he threw them back, put his helm over, and this time
gained the full width of the river into the wind. Looking aft,
Hornblower saw that the *Flame* was following her consort's
example. The lee shore seemed to come to meet them; it
seemed a very short time before the manœuvre would have to
be repeated, and Hornblower was relieved to see that the bend
was appreciably nearer.

It was at that moment that the Duke's head appeared above
the coaming as he climbed the little companion, and the royal

party began to swarm on deck again. Freeman looked with despair at Hornblower, who took the necessary decision. He fixed the nearest courtier—the equerry, it happened to be—with a look that cut short the laughing speech he was addressing to the lady at his side.

'It is not convenient for His Royal Highness and his suite to be on deck at present,' Hornblower said loudly.

The gay chatter stopped as if cut off with a knife; Hornblower looked at the crestfallen faces and was reminded of children again, spoiled children deprived of some minor pleasure.

'The management of the ship calls for too much attention,' went on Hornblower, to make his point quite clear. Freeman was already bellowing at the hands at the sheets.

'Very well, Sir 'Oratio,' said the Duke. 'Come, ladies. Come, gentlemen.'

He beat as dignified a retreat as possible, but the last courtier down the companion was sadly hustled by the rush of the hands across the deck.

'Up helm!' said Freeman to the steersman, and then, in the breathing space while they gathered way close-hauled, 'Shall I batten down, sir?'

The outrageous suggestion was made with a grin.

'No,' snapped Hornblower, in no mood for joking.

On the next tack *Porta Coeli* succeeded in weathering the point. Round she came and round; Freeman jibed her neatly, and once more with the wind on her quarter the brig was running free up the next reach, wooded hills on one side, fat meadow-land on the other.

At the next bend Rouen's cathedral towers were plain to the sight; at the one after that only a comparatively narrow neck of land separated them from the city, although there was still a long and beautiful curve of the river to navigate.

It was still early afternoon when they rounded the last bend and saw the whole city stretched before them, the island with its bridges, its wharves cluttered with river boats, the market hall across the quay, and the soaring Gothic towers which had looked down upon the burning of Joan of Arc. It was a tricky business anchoring there just below the town with the last of the flood still running; Hornblower had to take advantage of a minor bend in the stream to throw all aback and anchor by the stern, two cables' lengths farther from the city than he would have chosen in other circumstances. He scanned the city through his glass for signs of a deputation coming to greet them, and the Duke stood beside him, inclined to chafe at any delay.

'I'll have a boat, if you please, Mr Freeman,' Hornblower said at length. 'Will you pass the word for my coxswain?'

Crowds were already gathering on the quays to stare at the English ships, at the White Ensign and at the Bourbon lilies; it was twenty years since either had been seen there. There was quite a mass of people assembled when Brown laid the boat alongside the quay just below the bridge. Hornblower walked up the steps, eyed by the crowd. They were apathetic and silent, not like any French crowd he had seen or heard before. He caught sight of a man in uniform, a sergeant of *douaniers*.

'I wish to visit the Mayor,' he said.

'Yes, sir,' said the *douanier* respectfully.

'Call a carriage for me,' said Hornblower.

There was a little hesitation; the *douanier* looked about him doubtfully, but soon voices from the crowd began to make suggestions, and it was not long before a rattling hackney coach made its appearance. Hornblower climbed in, and they clattered off. The Mayor received him on the threshold of the

Hôtel de Ville, having hastened there to meet him from his desk as soon as he heard of his arrival.

'Where is the reception for His Royal Highness?' demanded Hornblower. 'Why have no salutes been fired? Why are the church bells not ringing?'

'Monsieur—Your Excellency——' The Mayor knew not quite what Hornblower's uniform and ribbon implied and wanted to be on the safe side. 'We did not know—we were not certain——'

'You saw the royal standard,' said Hornblower. 'You knew that His Royal Highness was on his way here from Le Havre.'

'There had been rumours, yes,' said the Mayor reluctantly. 'But——'

What the Mayor wanted to say was that he hoped the Duke would arrive not only with overpowering force but also would make an unassuming entrance so that nobody would have to commit themselves too definitely on the Bourbon side according him a welcome. And that was exactly what Hornblower had come to force him to do.

'His Royal Highness,' said Hornblower, 'is seriously annoyed. If you wish to regain his favour, and that of His Majesty the King who will follow him, you will make all the amends in your power. A deputation—you, all your councillors, all the notables, the Prefect and the Sub-prefect if they are still here, every person of position, in fact, must be on hand two hours from now to welcome Monseigneur when he lands.'

'Monsieur——'

'Note will be taken of who is present. And of who is absent,' said Hornblower. 'The church bells can begin to ring immediately.'

The Mayor tried to meet Hornblower's eyes. He was still in fear of Bonaparte, still terrified in case some reversal of fortune should leave him at Bonaparte's mercy, called to account for his actions in receiving the Bourbon. And, on the other hand, Hornblower knew well enough that if he could persuade the city to offer an open welcome, Rouen would think twice about changing sides again. He was determined upon winning allies for his cause.

'Two hours,' said Hornblower, 'will be ample for all preparations to be made, for the deputation to assemble, for the streets to be decorated, for quarters to be prepared for His Royal Highness and his suite.'

'Monsieur, you do not understand all that this implies,' protested the Mayor. 'It means——'

'It means that you are having to decide whether to enjoy the King's favour or not,' said Hornblower. 'That is the choice before you.'

Hornblower ignored the point that the Mayor was also having to decide whether or not to risk the guillotine at Bonaparte's hands.

'A wise man,' said Hornblower, meaningfully, 'will not hesitate a moment.'

So hesitant was the Mayor that Hornblower began to fear that he would have to use threats. He could threaten dire vengeance to-morrow or the next day when the advancing army should arrive; more effectively, he could threaten to knock the town to pieces immediately with his ships' guns, but that was not a threat he wanted to put into execution at all; it would be far from establishing the impression he wished to convey of a people receiving its rulers with acclamation after years of suffering under a tyrant.

'Time presses,' said Hornblower, looking at his watch.

'Very well,' said the Mayor, taking the decision which might mean life or death to him. 'I'll do it. What does Your Excellency suggest?'

It took only a matter of minutes to settle the details; Hornblower had learned from Hau much about arranging the public appearances of royalty. Then he took his leave, and drove back again to the quay through the silent crowds, to where the boat lay with Brown growing anxious about him. They had hardly pushed off into the stream when Brown cocked his ear. A church carillon had begun its chimes, and within a minute another had joined in. On the deck of the *Porta Coeli* the Duke listened to what Hornblower had to tell him. The city was making ready to welcome him.

And when they landed on the quay there was the assembly of notables, as promised; there were the carriages and the horses; there were the white banners in the streets. And there were the apathetic crowds, numbed with disaster. But it meant that Rouen was quiet during their stay there, the reception could at least have an appearance of gaiety, so that Hornblower went to bed each night worn out.

Hornblower turned his head on the pillow as the thumping on the door penetrated at last into his consciousness.

It was Dobbs, slippered and in his shirt-sleeves, his braces hanging by his thighs, his hair in a mop. He held a candle in one hand and a despatch in the other.

'It's over!' he said. 'Boney's abdicated! Blucher's in Paris!'

So there it was. Victory; the end of twenty years of war. Hornblower sat up and blinked at the candle.

'The Duke must be told,' he said. He was gathering his thoughts. 'Is the King still in England? What does that despatch say?'

He got himself out of bed in his nightshirt.

'All right, Dobbs,' said Hornblower. 'I'll be with you in five minutes. Send to wake the Duke and warn him that I am about to come to him.'

The Duke kept him waiting fifteen minutes in the drawing-room of the residence of the departed Prefect where he had been installed. He heard the news with his council round him, and with royal stoicism showed no sign of emotion.

'What about the usurper?' was his first question after hearing what Hornblower had to say.

'His future is partially decided, Your Royal Highness. He has been promised a minor sovereignty,' said Hornblower. It sounded absurd to him as he said it.

'And His Majesty, my uncle?'

'The despatch does not say, Your Royal Highness. Doubtless His Majesty will leave England now. Perhaps he is already on his way.'

'We must be at the Tuileries to receive him.'

Hornblower sat in his sitting-room in the Hôtel Meurice in Paris a month later rereading the crackling parchment document that had arrived for him the previous day. The wording of it might be called as gratifying as the purport of it, to one who cared for such things.

As the grandeur and stability of the British Empire depend chiefly upon knowledge and experience in maritime affairs, We esteem those worthy of the highest honours who, acting under Our influence, exert themselves in maintaining Our dominion over the sea. It is for this reason that We have determined to advance to the degree of Peerage Our trusty and well beloved Sir Horatio Hornblower, Knight of the Most Honourable Order of the Bath, who, being descended from an ancient family in Kent, and educated from his youth in the sea service, hath through several posts arrived to high station and command in Our navy, by the strength of his own abilities, and a merit distinguished by Us, in the many

*important services, which he has performed with remark-
able fidelity, courage and success. In the late vigorous
wars, which raged so many years in Europe; wars fruit-
ful of naval combats and expeditions; there was scarce
any action of consequence wherein he did not bear a
principal part, nor were any dangers or difficulties too
great, but he surmounted them by his exquisite conduct,
and a good fortune that never failed him.*

*'It is just, therefore, that We should distinguish with
higher titles a subject who has so eminently served Us
and his country, both as monuments of his own merit,
and to influence others into a love and pursuit of virtue.*

So now he was a Peer of the Realm, a Baron of the United
Kingdom, Lord Hornblower of Smallbridge, County of Kent.
There were only two or three other examples in history of a
naval officer being raised to the peerage before attaining flag
rank.